Foreword

When visiting professional associates in, e.g., Europe, or in French-speaking Canada, I have often been amazed to realize that they are as well-read in the American professional literature as we are. On the other hand, because of my language handicap (English only), I seldom read professional material that originally appeared in other languages, and only infrequently see professional material which appeared first in another language which has been translated into English. I suspect that many of my American colleagues are in the same situation. This is unfortunate, since many of our French-Canadian and European colleagues have a great deal to contribute to our understanding of instructional technology, training, cognitive psychology, and related topics. Fortunately, many of them also publish in English, but I always fear that we are missing much of value that does not appear in English.

Nick Eastmond has provided a valuable service by teaming with Robert Brien to bring to an American audience a work which appeared originally in French. We have the good fortune to enjoy the work of Robert Brien, which otherwise would be limited to a French-speaking audience. The excellent original work has been updated and refined with reader questions and exercises, a comprehensive glossary, and an expanded index.

The topic of cognitive science and instruction is a timely one. Professional meetings recently have been filled with papers dedicated to the proposition that training and instructional development could be considerably enhanced by more careful attention to cognitive science. In this book Brien and Eastmond have summarized some of the most pertinent hypotheses and findings of cognitive science, and have attempted to suggest some implications that these findings might have for the design and presentation of instructional materials. In many cases, they have clarified cognitive science so that it can be more easily understood and applied by those who have not studied this area in depth.

They have then suggested some general principles for instruction that the application of these principles imply.

The authors have provided valuable insights which should whet the appetite of the reader in a way that will entice one to search more deeply for the insights to instruction provided by research and theory in cognitive science.

M. David Merrill
Utah State University

Preface

Few authors can literally claim to have developed an entirely original line of thought. Most, having been taught by leaders in their discipline, have gone on to enrich their formal knowledge with practical experiences or with additional communication. This work is no exception, it being based upon work done by Robert Gagné (Florida State University), Donald A. Norman, David Rumelhart, and George Mandler (University of California, San Diego); Jean-François Richard, Guy Dehnière, Serge Baudet, and Jean-Michel Hoc (University of Paris); and Jean-François Le Ny and Michel Denis (University of Paris-South). Acquired concepts have been amplified in workshops, conferences, and seminars held in France and in the United States, thanks to the contributions of these researchers.

This book sets forth ideas from cognitive science that can be applied in the design of instruction. It is not itself a guide for the design of instruction. The application of cognitive science to the design of instruction is still in its infancy, and the development of a *fully prescriptive guide* is still in the future. This book is oriented toward the prospective instructional designer or those presently practicing in the field who want to enrich their work with insights from cognitive science.

The present work owes much to constructive critiques by colleagues and friends who have read, entirely or in part, various versions of the text. In particular, Michel Denis and Jean-Michel Hoc, cited above, as well as Béatrice Galinon-Mélénec (University of Bordeaux), Renane Saumurçay (University of Paris), Raymond Paquin (University of Québec at Trois Rivières), Jacques Lapointe (Laval University), Philippe Marton (Laval University), Paul Goulet (Laval University), Yves Poisson (Laval University), Philippe Duchastel (Laval University), Madeleine Perron (Laval University), Marc Maurice (Association ONFOC, Haute-de-Seine), Maria Grazzia Quieti (F.A.O.), Danielle Marquis, Monique Aubin, and Victoire Lévesque are to be thanked for their helpful contributions.

For the English version, the help of M. David Merrill and Margaret Dyreson (both at Utah State University) and editorial and research assistance from Inhae (Annie) Kim and Jay Huber have been invaluable.

One should not forget those persons who daily allow a testing of the instructional aspects of this text—the students—without whom this work could not have been completed. Unfortunately, a complete listing here is impossible, but mention should be made of the collaborative efforts of Hélène Beaulieu, Martin Robert, Nicole Lapointe, and most especially Denyse Pépin. Members of a current-issues seminar providing formative feedback for the English language version were Matthew Dirks, Catherine Elwell, Ehr-Ping Fang, Kathryn Gustafson, Michelle O'Brien, and Allen Rowe.

And, finally, a note of thanks is due to our employers, Laval University and Utah State University, for furnishing through a variety of sources the opportunities for acquiring the understanding necessary to put together this volume.

In the chapters that follow, the reader will be exposed to personal interpretations of research completed in cognitive science over the last four decades and an extension of these ideas into the world of instruction. This volume does not claim to be a synthesis of research completed to date, but rather, through the use of references to important works, a guide to follow in deepening understanding of this promising field of human understanding. Some of the chapters following are adaptations of articles published previously or presentations given. It goes without saying that the ideas and the hypotheses advanced are solely the responsibility of the two authors and not those of the persons contributing to the book's preparation.

Robert Brien
Université Laval —Québec, Canada

Nick Eastmond
Utah State University—Logan, Utah, USA

September 1993

Table of Contents

Cognitive Science and Instruction

Chapter 1

Introduction
to Cognitive Science

Generally we imagine scientific progress as a series of rational steps along an ascending path; in fact, it is more often a series of zigzags, almost more surprising, at times, than the evolution of political thought.

Arthur Koestler, *Bricks to Babel*, 1981

Historical Perspective

In 1979, researchers in the areas of cognitive psychology, artificial intelligence, linguistics, and philosophy gathered at the University of California, San Diego. The intent of this meeting was to inaugurate a new science, "cognitive science," with the stated goal of understanding intelligent behavior (see Norman, 1981, for a summary of this colloquium).[1]

Important work had been completed in cognitive sciences[2] well before 1979 (see Gardner, 1985, & Varela, 1989, for an engaging historical view of these developments). Moving beyond the taboos of the behaviorist school of thought, highly influential in the United States since the 1940's, researchers of cognition became interested in the study of the physical makeup of human memory and the ways in which information is stored, coded, and utilized by the human brain. According to Herbert Simon, one of the participants at the La Jolla meeting, one must return to the year 1956 to be present at the real birth of cognitive science (Simon, 1981a). In fact, it was during that year that Miller published his now-famous work on the properties of short-term memory (Miller, 1956), that Chomsky presented his analysis of the properties of transformational grammar (Chomsky, 1956), and that Bruner, Goodnow, and Austin (1956) examined man's cognitive strategies in the acquisition

---

[1] For Herbert Simon, one of the pioneers of cognitive science and Nobel Prize winner in economics in 1978, cognitive science realigns fields such as cognitive psychology, artificial intelligence, philosophy, and linguistics (Simon, 1981a). Other researchers suggest the inclusion of the neurosciences in this group (see "Debate on the direction of the Association for Cognitive Research" in the member bulletin, *Intellectica* 1984). This last position is adopted in the present text.

[2] Cognitive scientists generally use the expressions "cognitive science" or "the cognitive sciences," which they consider the partial or full integration of the sciences previously mentioned. We will utilize both of these expressions in this text.

of concepts. It was also during this same year that Newell and Simon first put forward their computer program, the logic theorist, which imitated human problem-solving processes (Newell & Simon, 1956).

Since that remarkable year, interest in cognitive science has continued to grow: several societies have been founded, numerous books and articles published, and programs of study offered in universities. Cognitive science is of major intellectual interest in the 1990's.

Goals and Premises of This Book

In spite of the recent progress of research in cognitive sciences, applications of this knowledge to the realm of instruction remain limited. The present limitations are partly attributable to the abstract nature of extant cognitive models and partly to the tendency of researchers to study only one aspect of a given phenomenon at a time. Also, we must consider the development of a science and its application as two distinct tasks; and, in the final analysis, the task of applying the principles of cognitive science to the design of instructional activities should rely upon the educational psychologist or the instructional technologist (Gagné, 1980).

It is in view of the perceived need to apply cognitive science principles to instruction that this book was written. Beginning with the idea that, in order to act effectively on a system, one must know the system well, we will describe the important components of the human information processing system. After completing this description, we will offer basic prescriptions useful in guiding the designer and the facilitator of instructional activities. Another objective of this book, no less important, is to encourage readers to follow up on the references proposed and thereby to deepen their knowledge of this unfolding domain.

The book is based upon a number of premises or working hypotheses. The *first premise*, to which we have alluded in the preceding pages, suggests that, to work effectively, the designer of instructional activities and the teacher must have the most accurate mental model possible of persons destined for instruction. These professions must know how a human being stores information, forms representations, and utilizes the information (see Anderson, 1986, regarding the importance of using appropriate mental models; also Johnson-Laird, 1983, and Gentner & Stevens, 1983). This model of the learner used by the designer and trainer[3] should also furnish information about the role of affect (feelings) in processing information.

The need for this model is apparent. An analogy in modern medicine would be to ask what would happen if, in the middle of open-heart surgery, the surgeon performing the operation were momentarily deprived of any mental model of the functioning of the human heart. The results would likely be disastrous. Having an accurate model in mind is absolutely essential.

For Herbert Simon, the information processing system of an adaptive organism plays a similar role to that of a thermostat, constantly comparing reality with its pre-set expectations. When the information processing system finds itself lacking in some regard, it lays out plans for changing reality in the direction of its expectations. This viewpoint constitutes the foundation upon which our model of the learner is built and serves as the *second premise of* this book: namely, that the learner will attempt to change reality to meet his expectations. Simon's position is well stated as follows:

> Given a desired condition and an actual one, the task of an adaptive organism is to evaluate the gap existing between the two situations, and to find a process that allows for the closing of that gap.

> (Simon, 1981b, p. 223)

A *third premise* is suggested by psychologist Jerome Bruner in his book *Toward a Theory of Instruction* (1967). According to this pioneer in cognitive science, if one wishes to have a useful theory of instruction, the theory must be *prescriptive* and not purely *descriptive*. In other words, the theory cannot simply describe mental processes that enter into learning, but must suggest or prescribe ways of activating processes so that learning can occur. Because the theoretical base of cognitive science is not yet complete, we cannot as yet deduce full principles. Far from dictating a theory of teaching—our goal is more modest—this book

---

[3] This book is directed to a variety of professionals involved in education of all kinds. Recognizing that differences do exist, but wanting to address various professional groups, a convention used throughout this text is to use the terms "trainer," "instructor," and "teacher" interchangeably.

proposes for the designer or facilitator of instructional activities a series of suggestions to guide the accomplishment of tasks. Our applications will be in the context of educational technology, giving the steps of designing and conducting instructional activities. The suggestions that we provide will apply to the motivation of the learners, the formulation of instructional objectives, the structuring of content for instructional activities, the choice of appropriate teaching methods, and the evaluation of results.[4]

A *fourth premise* is suggested by the work of Romiszowski (1980), who deplores the belief, unfortunately widespread, that the design and conducting of instructional activities requires only the simple application of well-established formulas. While the use of appropriate techniques can guide in designing and conducting instructional activities, successfully carrying out these activities relies in large measure on the creativity and problem-solving capacity of the trainer. For us, planning and conducting instruction require establishing a set of instructional activities that help the learner to transform an already existing cognitive structure into one that is more appropriate. This task, as we will realize in the next chapters, presupposes problem-solving skills on the part of the instructional designer or teacher.

Structure of the Book

If, as Simon has suggested, the task of an adaptive organism is to compare its present situation with its expectations and then to search for a process to bridge the gap, it is important at this stage to note that, when this organism is a human being, the person must possess, at a minimum, functions or mechanisms that allow him or her to:

    a.   be motivated to accomplish these tasks;

    b.   form representations about existing and desired conditions;

    c.   accomplish tasks likely to bridge the gap between these conditions; and

---

[4]   This book is oriented toward the perspective of instructional technology (see Stolovitch & Larocque, 1983; Lachance, Lapointe, & Marton, 1979; Brien, 1989). In instructional technology, a distinction is made between tasks related to the *design* of activities and those related to the *teaching* of them.

> d. acquire the necessary competencies to accomplish these tasks.

Subsequent chapters deal with these functions, in the order just suggested; see Figure 1.

Figure 1. Themes covered in each chapter.

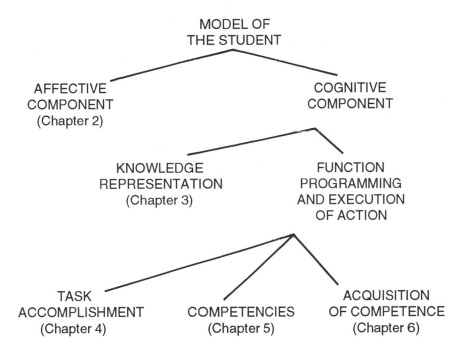

After establishing the framework for our study in this first chapter, we examine in Chapter 2 the driving role played by affect, or feelings, in learning. Our belief is that motivation is a key element of learning, often neglected both in theory and in practice. We will describe the role of individual needs, expectations, emotions, attitudes, values, and thus motivation in learning.

In Chapter 3, we explore the task of knowledge representation in human memory. We will describe the role of mnemonic structures, called "schemas," used for storing, as well as representing and utilizing information. This examination of the ways of representing knowledge will lead us, at the end of the chapter, to formulate recommendations for structuring instructional activities.

In Chapter 4 we analyze the process of planning and executing an action, following the perception of a gap between an existing and a desired situation. We will deal with the cognitive processes necessary to accomplish a complex task and will propose a hierarchical model for task accomplishment, based mainly upon Luria's theory (1973, 1980).

Next, in Chapter 5, we will examine the notion of human competency. A human competency is defined as the set of procedures and sub-procedures activated during the accomplishment of a given task. When speaking of one such unit, we term it a competency. We will end this chapter with a classification of human competencies and will propose a method for formulating instructional objectives that takes mental activity into account as the basis for performance.

Whenever an individual does not possess the competence necessary to adequately complete a task, he or she generally engages in activities called learning. The processing of information then undertaken aims at transforming this existing cognitive structure, the cause of perceived incompetence, into a cognitive structure more adapted to the task at hand. We will raise the questions in Chapter 6 about the manner of acquiring human competence, insisting particularly on processes during the assembly and refining of competency.

Finally, in Chapter 7, we will suggest a simple application of the concepts proposed throughout the book.

Questions: Chapter 1

For review: [5]

(1) What is the basic response of an adaptive organism upon perceiving a gap between reality and its desires? For a human being in this situation, what are the four prerequisites for a person to be able to so respond?

(2) What benefits can be realized when designers and teachers have accurate mental models of the targeted learners?

For further reflection:

(1) What are the consequences of a purely descriptive learning theory? Is it possible to have a complete, purely descriptive theory of mental processes to which prescriptions cannot be attached by inference?

(2) The theory of behaviorism suggests that a theory of instruction will consider only outside stimuli and observable responses made by an organism. What will be the differences between an instructional design based upon cognitive science principles and one suggested by the principles of behaviorism?

---

[5] Suggested answers to the "Questions for Review" are provided in the section following the Glossary at the end of the book. The "Questions for Further Reflection" are left to the reader without commentary.

Chapter 2

Affect and Cognition[1]

The most important art of the master is to bring out the joy in work and in understanding.

Albert Einstein, *The World as I See It*, **1949**

---

[1] See also Brien (1987).

Introduction

The designer and the trainer have an ingrained tendency to consider only the intellectual side of the person receiving instruction. They frequently neglect the fact that the individual learner has needs, desires, emotions, attitudes, and values, and that motivation plays a key role in the processing of information presented. The consequences of this omission are unfortunate, frequently resulting in instructional activities offering little stimulation, and over time creating an aversion to learning. It is a positive attitude toward learning that must be developed throughout instruction. Even though this is an unusual position for most cognitive scientists to take, this chapter treats the complementary roles of feelings and cognition as a necessary beginning for learning.

To fully comprehend the role of feelings in learning, it is necessary to leave the classroom, school, or training center, and to consider the learner in natural surroundings. In the first part of this chapter, we will return to the model of adaptation of an organism to its environment put forward in the first chapter. To this model we will add elements of theories by Ausubel (1968), Bower (1975), Maslow (1970), Lindsay and Norman (1977), and Mandler (1984). The new model emphasizes the effects of individual needs, expectations, emotions, attitudes, values, and motivation on learning. In light of a model proposed by Keller (1983) and Keller and Burkman (1993), and keeping in mind the ideas of Nuttin (1980), we will propose recommendations for guiding designers and instructors in the preparation of motivating instructional activities.

Theoretical Foundations

Adaptation of the Individual to the Surrounding Environment

The model proposed by Simon, as cited in the previous chapter, while very powerful, only partially describes the steps taken by the human being to adapt to the surrounding environment. To complete this effort, it is necessary to add an affective dimension.

Needs and Expectations

Several classifications of human needs have been proposed during the last two decades (Maslow, 1970; Keller, 1983; Nuttin, 1980). While some specific elements of these classifications may be called into question, their authors seem to have agreed upon the same basic principle, which can be simply stated as follows: *most activities or behaviors of the individual are oriented toward the satisfaction of needs.*

Abraham Maslow (1970) proposed five major categories of needs: (1) physiological needs, to include hunger, thirst, sex, and other bodily needs; (2) safety and security needs, to include protection against physical and psychological threat; (3) social needs, to include friendship, affection, belonging, and acceptance by others; (4) ego needs, to include self-esteem, reputation, recognition, and attention; and (5) self-actualization, to include self-realization, leading the person to develop his or her full potential.[2]

Innate or acquired, these needs move the individual to a constant search, conscious or unconscious, for satisfying conditions or states. We say that mental representation of these satisfying conditions or these states constitutes the primary expectations or goals[3] of the person.

---

[2] For Maslow, these needs are hierarchical. In order to satisfy the needs of a higher level, the needs of a lower level must be taken care of. We do not retain this aspect of his theory in the material that follows, as we concentrate on the specific notion of need. Along the same lines, we believe that other needs, such as aesthetic or spiritual ones, can coexist as well.

[3] The expression *goal-object* is often used to characterize primary expectations.

In this context, we suggest that there is not necessarily a one-to-one correspondence between the expectations or goals of the individual and his or her needs. Frequently, a given situation can satisfy several needs all at once.

Thus, a surprise party can be perceived differently by the person(s) being surprised: one person will see it as an occasion to satisfy physiological needs; someone else will consider it as a sign of affection; another as a sign of respect. A fourth person may view the event as an occasion to enhance personal development (enriching discussions, new acquaintances, etc.). Finally, and probably for most people, this kind of event will satisfy all of these needs, at least to some extent.

Chains of Expectations

We also believe in the existence, in each human being, of intermediate expectations or sub-goals subordinated to the goal-objects or primary expectations discussed earlier. For example, the obtaining of a diploma in a certain domain can constitute a subordinate goal allowing the fulfillment of a goal, in this case, approval from others or job security. To get a grade of "A" in a course that is part of a full program of study can constitute a subordinate sub-goal of the larger goal of obtaining a diploma. Finally, the mastery of competency X, in a certain lesson of a course in this program, also constitutes a sub-goal subsumed under the previous goal of obtaining a diploma. We can thus use the expression "chain of expectations" to characterize the set requiring E_1, E_2, E_3, ..., E_n of intermediate expectations or sub-goals oriented toward the attainment of a primary expectation or a particular "Goal X."

We are thus led to acknowledge the existence, within the human being, of a constant process for problem resolution, by building chains of expectations subordinate to the attainment of a goal-object. The process of adaptation of a human being to his or her environment seems to us to be an activity characterized by the constant elaboration of chains of expectations which, themselves, are capable of satisfying the fundamental needs of the individual. (See Wilensky, 1983, for an interesting theory of these goals.)

Links Among Needs, Expectancies, and Emotions

Keeping in mind the argument of the preceding section, we can hypothesize that human beings continually present for themselves, in conscious or unconscious fashion, the desired conditions, satisfactory states, or goals toward which they strive to meet personal needs.

In addition, consciously or unconsciously, the person continually compares his or her representation of the existing situation[4] with that of the desired situation. When the existing situation differs from the desired one, a physiological reaction on the part of the organism follows (see Lindsay & Norman, 1977; Mandler, 1984), characterized in part by the secretion of adrenaline and by the acceleration of pulse and breathing. Depending upon the intensity of the physiological reaction and the cognitive evaluation of the resulting condition, the person experiences positive or negative emotions[5] of strong or weak intensity and of one quality or another, depending upon the originating need.[6] The central part of Figure 2 illustrates the process of an emergence of an emotion.

This process can be summed up as follows: (a) the needs of the individual bring about the elaboration of expectations, leading to the formulation of goals; (b) if there is a gap between expectations and the existing situation, there is a physiological reaction; (c) there is then a positive or negative cognitive evaluation of the situation; and (d) this evaluation causes an agreeable or a disagreeable emotion.

---

[4] Representation of the existing situation encompasses the representation of the external situation and that of the internal situation of the organism, a condition that some authors (Neisser, 1976) have termed "proprioception." Representation of the external situation consists in the individual's perception of external stimuli. Representation of the internal situation consists in part of the perception of the availability or nonavailability of a plan and the perception of the existing physiological state. These internal and external representations follow the activation of the person's schemas, and are thus highly subjective.

[5] For an engaging review of modern theories of the emotions, see *Emotion: Theory, Research, and Experience* in the collection by Plutchik & Kellerman (1980); and *Emotions, Cognition and Behavior*, by Izard, Kogan, & Zajonc (1984).

[6] Mandler (1984) describes the process of the emergence of an emotion, but he does not tie the quality of the emotion to the individual's needs. Koestler (1968) suggests such a linkage.

Figure 2. Possible connections between needs, emotions, and attitudes.

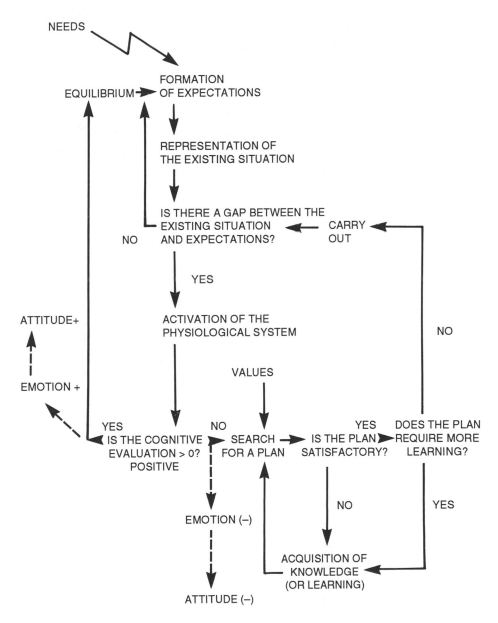

To illustrate this process of the emergence of an emotion, let us imagine the case where we try out a restaurant based upon someone's recommendation. We come with certain expectations regarding the food and the service (desired condition). Once seated, we can see that the service leaves something to be desired and that the food being served is rather mediocre or was prepared under less than hygienic conditions. There is thus a gap between our expectations and the existing situation. This gap brings about the activation of the physiological system and secretion of adrenaline, followed by a cognitive evaluation of the situation. Since in this case the evaluation is negative, we experience an unpleasant emotion. In another case, the reality could have surpassed our expectations, and a pleasant emotion would have followed.

Emotions from Reminiscence and from Anticipation

In this context, it is interesting to note that the proposed model explains, in part, the phenomenon of the emergence of emotions before or after the actual event, by reminiscence or by anticipation. In effect, we can postulate that in the case of reminiscence, the individual can experience in the present context agreeable or disagreeable emotions encountered in an earlier time period. We can consider that in the present moment the individual represents a situation experienced in the past (previously existing situation), that the person compares this memory with prior expectations (previously desired situation), and that a pleasant or unpleasant emotion experienced in the past is lived out in the present. To illustrate this phenomenon, we could imagine a student who, in remembering a past school failure, feels unhappiness from it. To simplify things, we can consider that this student simulates, in the present, the situation lived through at the time of that school failure. We can imagine that the person can recollect previous desires for success, as well as the news of having failed (the previously existing condition), and that as the two situations are compared, the physiological system is activated, the cognitive evaluation comes up negative, and an unpleasant emotion results. As we all know from personal experience, it is possible to have mixed emotions, partly positive and partly negative.

In the same way, it is possible that the process of an emotion's emergence may be activated by the simulation of events yet to come. In this case, the individual anticipates the eventuality of a situation not yet experienced. This evaluation can then result in pleasant or unpleasant emotions in the present, depending upon whether the anticipated existing situation surpasses or falls short of the individual's expectations. As an example, we might imagine pleasant emotions experienced in anticipation of a trip to a foreign country. In this case, the person's expectations color the possible eventual situation, going beyond simple desires and bringing with them pleasant emotions. Unfortunately, reality often falls short of our expectations, and the emotions actually experienced by the traveler are not always as pleasant as the anticipations.[7]

Connections Between Emotions and Attitudes

We now consider the important influence exerted by favorable or unfavorable recollections on the decision of whether or not to perform a given task in the future. The memory of pleasant or unpleasant emotions experienced during the accomplishment of a given task will determine the positive or negative attitude toward subsequent accomplishment of this task.

Thus, in addition to the knowledge required for the accomplishment of diverse tasks of the sort undertaken daily by the individual, we must add a positive or negative valence related to pleasant or unpleasant memories from emotions previously experienced while accomplishing these tasks. We can expect that at the moment of activation of the necessary knowledge to accomplish a given task, an emotion already experienced is

---

[7] Here we must leave to the reader to consider the subjectivity of the emotions experienced. In the face of certain identical events, some people experience pleasant emotions, while others will feel unpleasant ones. It all depends upon the person's desires and the representation of the existing situation that the person makes for himself or herself. These representations of wishes and of the existing situation depend, as previously mentioned, on the schemas possessed by each person. With practice, it is often possible to change from unpleasant to pleasant emotions. This can be done by diminishing or moderating one's wishes, and dedramatizing the impact of an existing situation. This is what a friend does when, seeing us in a predicament, the person invites us to have a chat, a meal together, etc. Most of the time, by talking our problems through with us, the friend can bring us "back to reality": helping us take into account our idealism (our wishes are often too grandiose) or our tendencies to overdramatize an existing situation.

activated by the individual, and this condition incites or inhibits the accomplishment of the task. We can now understand more clearly the definition of an attitude as a "disposition of the organism to choose this or that type of activity" (Gagné, 1984; Krathwohl, Bloom, & Masia, 1964).

We understand also, in reference to the example of the restaurant cited earlier, the importance for an establishment wishing to increase its clientele to leave its customers with a pleasant emotional experience, since these emotions will engender a positive attitude toward the establishment. In instruction, we should realize the importance for the student participant to experience pleasant emotions in the act of learning. In the short term, these emotions will bring about positive attitudes toward the particular content and toward the tasks being accomplished and, in the long term, positive attitudes toward learning in general.

Human Motivation

Given this frame of reference, several definitions of human motivation are possible. Human motivation can be considered as "the effort that the individual is ready to invest for the accomplishment of a given task," or "the effort that the person is ready to furnish to change an existing situation to a desired situation." In referring to the work of Nuttin (1980), Bloom (1976), and Keller (1983), we can postulate that motivation is mainly a function of the intensity of needs felt by the individual, of the magnitude of the task to be completed, and of the number of previously successful accomplishments of the task completed. An individual will be motivated to accomplish a certain task if a payoff (eventual satisfaction of needs) is evident. A person will also be motivated to accomplish the task if its completion seems feasible and if success has already been experienced in the past in accomplishing analogous tasks. These considerations are relative to the needs of the individual: knowing the person's desires, emotions, and attitudes help us to determine the role of learning in the individual's life.

The Place of Learning

To bridge the gap between an existing situation and one's expectations, the individual must take certain actions. As Miller, Galanter, and Pribam (1960) have suggested, and as will be discussed in Chapter 4, these actions are guided by plans which may exist in the person's repertoire or which may be developed for the particular circumstance. In the ideal situation, the person possesses a plan of action allowing the realization of sub-goals and the final goal-object (i.e., the final goal or desired condition). In other cases the person does not possess such a plan but must work to develop one. In doing so, he or she becomes involved in problem resolution and is influenced by personal values (see Figure 2). During problem resolution, knowledge acquisition or learning takes place. Thus, learning appears as an activity which indirectly permits the individual to satisfy fundamental needs and, in turn, to adapt to the environment. A synthesized view of the progressive adaptation of the person to a particular environment is suggested by Figure 3.

To satisfy an expectation or a particular goal X, the individual must pass through the intermediate stages or sub-goals S_1, S_2, S_3, ... S_n. To complete these sub-goals, the person must carry out tasks T_1, T_2, T_3 ... T_n. In the case where the competency to complete these tasks is lacking, the person must take the path that we have chosen to call learning. The individual undertakes the assembly and the refinement of competencies C_1, C_2, C_3 ... C_n that permit accomplishment of tasks T_1, T_2, T_3, ... T_n. Thus, we can consider competencies as being themselves sub-goals, the attainment of which facilitates the accomplishment of tasks which permit the realization of goals and thus the satisfaction of the person's needs. Learning and the needs of the individual can thus be linked by means of the chain illustrated in Figure 4.

Affect and Learning

The role of affect in learning now is more clear. We can postulate that the affective processes coming into play during the accomplishment of a learning task are the same as those present during the accomplishment of any task in general. During the accomplishment of a learning task, we see the development of expectations or goals (desired competence), the representation of the existing situation (incompetence), and the

Figure 3. Learning as a means of attaining one's expectations.

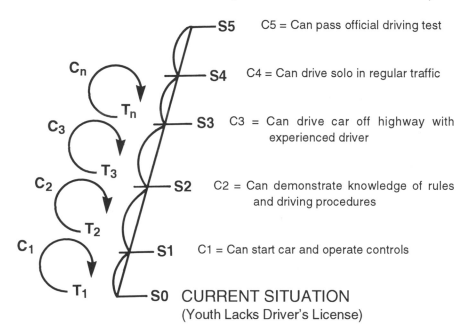

EXPECTATION X
(Youth Receives Driver's License)

S5   C5 = Can pass official driving test

S4   C4 = Can drive solo in regular traffic

S3   C3 = Can drive car off highway with experienced driver

S2   C2 = Can demonstrate knowledge of rules and driving procedures

S1   C1 = Can start car and operate controls

S0   CURRENT SITUATION
(Youth Lacks Driver's License)

Si = situation Ci = competence Ti = tasks

evaluation of the difference existing between the present situation and the goal (the need). Once this gap has been perceived, there is a physiological reaction on the part of the organism, and an evaluation, resulting in pleasant or unpleasant emotions. Subsequently, the emotions experienced during learning bring about positive or negative attitudes toward the subject under study or the task that must eventually be executed. Continuing this line of reasoning, the individual who is motivated is one that is ready to invest the necessary effort (in terms of mental operations to execute) to change his or her cognitive structure. The new structure then permits the accomplishment of a given task and, eventually, the satisfaction of personal needs. As is the case in the accomplishment of everyday tasks, the individual motivated toward

Figure 4. Linkages between learning tasks and the satisfaction of needs.

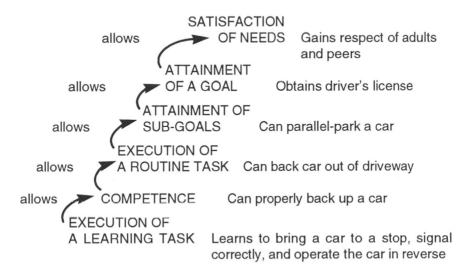

learning is the one for whom needs are considerable, for whom the size of the task appears reasonable, and whose experience in the past relative to the accomplishment of analogous tasks is positive.

Instructional Applications

In the first part of this chapter, we emphasized the relationships among needs, expectations, values, emotions, attitudes, and motivation. We indicated that acquired competencies bring about, in either the short or long term, the satisfaction of the person's needs, because competencies permit the accomplishment of given tasks. The cognitive perspective taken helps in the implementation of stimulating learning activities. In the following section, we will be particularly interested in ways to design stimulating instructional activities and in ways to help learners acquire particular attitudes favorable toward learning.

Motivation of the Learner

In the previous sections, we defined "motivation to learn" as the effort that the individual is ready to invest to change an existing cognitive structure into one more appropriate. We can postulate that *this effort is a function of at least three important factors: the intensity of the needs felt by the individual, the size of the learning task, and the attitude held toward this task.* We will now formulate a set of recommendations to assist the instructional designer, teacher, or trainer to maximize the influence of these three factors in an instructional situation and thus enhance the learner's motivation. These recommendations are derived from the discussion in this chapter and are based within the framework provided by motivational theories of Keller (1983), Martin and Briggs (1986), and Nuttin (1980). We will conclude the chapter by formulating additional suggestions more particularly adapted to the development of attitudes.

Motivation to Learn and Individual Needs

Help the learner to establish links between the competence to be acquired and the satisfaction of needs.

Since most human activities, including learning, are oriented toward the satisfaction of needs, the importance of the trainer's helping the learner to identify the links existing between the acquisition of a particular competency and the satisfaction of needs cannot be overemphasized. These linkages can be established by encouraging the learner to construct the appropriate chaining of expectations.

Depending upon the place of the learner in completing the particular lesson, course, or instructional program, it is possible to lead the learner to form various chains of expectations. At the beginning of a course, the teacher can explain the significance of the goal or goals of the course and the advantages to be obtained from completing these goals. Throughout the course, the teacher can make explicit the links between the accomplishment of the various learning tasks and the acquisition of a particular competency.

It would be erroneous to conclude that only verbal means can be used to make explicit the chains of appropriate expectations. A slide-show, a video, or a field trip illustrating the tasks involved in the acquisition of given competencies can constitute activities promoting the formation of chaining of expectations.

*Use methods of teaching that will permit the
satisfaction of individual needs.*

For most adults it is relatively easy to understand the links existing between learning, competence, tasks, goals, and need satisfaction. The adult understands that a certain course will bring about more employment security, that a certain diploma will bring more self-esteem and more respect from others, or that a certain activity will help satisfy personal curiosity. However, this is not always the case for the child or adolescent who is engaged in obtaining competencies to be used at some future date.

Fortunately, this problem can be resolved in part by the choice of methods of instruction involving activities linked to need satisfaction. Use of tournaments or educational games can build competition, which, if conducted within the bounds of good sportsmanship, can lead to self-esteem from pride in accomplishment. Learning in pairs or small groups can build upon the needs for friendship and self-esteem. The project method encourages self-expression and may satisfy social needs, particularly when a group project is involved. Laboratory methods, when used properly, build curiosity. Certain forms of individualized instruction encourage curiosity and individual attainment. Because the activities involved in these methods are tied to the possible satisfaction of fundamental needs, they promote the acquisition of particular competencies. Appendix A lists a large number of alternative modes of instruction.

Vary the stimuli and the methods of instruction.

We have examined the consequences of the learner's perceiving a positive or negative gap between a desired and an actual situation, leaving until now an analysis of the condition where the existing situation is perceived as equivalent to the situation desired. This case can be considered as an absence of stimulation for the individual. Researchers have demonstrated that the absence of stimulation, which they can simulate to some extent through the continual repetition of the same stimulus, leads to various psychological states, ranging from weariness to hallucinations. Unfortunately, this same state of weariness is seen all too often in learning when the stimuli presented and the methods of instruction are not varied sufficiently. Thus, in the design and presentation of instructional activities, it is essential that learning activities be varied and that different teaching methods be used.

Motivation and Size of the Learning Task

Present challenging learning activities.

Several researchers interested in the problems of human motivation have emphasized the importance of a state of dissatisfaction as a spur to action. According to Beer and Erl (1973), "All creative action accomplished by man derives from dissatisfaction with an existing state that he wishes to change in a positive way." In practice, the generation of plans enabling the bridging of a gap between an existing and a desired situation does not occur unless a certain dissatisfaction is felt strongly by the individual.[8]

Attend to prerequisite skills.

In many cases, the difficulty of a learning task can be attributed to the absence of prerequisite knowledge or skills on the part of the student (thus emphasizing the importance of instruction that takes into account prerequisites and where the content is closely structured). The minimal or negligible motivation encountered in students weak in math is most often due to the lack of mastery of the needed prerequisites and frequently a history of negative emotion associated with the subject. In certain cases, the size of the learning task is so great as to require years to catch up.

---

[8] This phenomenon can be at least partially explained by taking into account the person's needs for self-esteem and self-actualization. In most cases, we can assume that the individual will avoid a task for which the accomplishment has few chances of satisfying basic needs—thus avoiding failure if the individual sees the task as impossible, or avoiding involvement if the task is viewed as having negligible importance.

Motivation and Positive Attitudes Toward Learning

Design activities that elicit pleasant emotions.

Part of the challenge of effective teaching is designing activities that bring about pleasant emotions. As teachers, we should consider which activities to include to bring about the desired emotion. Most of the time during learning, an individual will experience pleasant emotions as he or she perceives progress toward the mastery of a given competency. In many cases, we can compare these favorable emotions to the phenomenon of positive reinforcement as described in the theory of operant conditioning.[9] These reinforcements are produced as a result of responses furnished by the student to exercises or problems during the attainment of an objective or during the completion of a unit or lesson. A correct answer acknowledged by a caring teacher can be reinforcing, as can the recognition of a correct response in a computer environment. The high probability of pleasant emotions can be foreseen by the person interacting with the system and prompt the effort required on the part of the learner to bring the condition about. In addition, the attainment of these emotions eventually develops positive attitudes toward learning itself.

In summary, the representation on the part of the individual of the existing situation has two principal components: one external and the other internal. The internal component resides in the information possessed by the learner, allowing the generation of plans capable of meeting his or her personal needs. The importance of students' adopting a positive attitude toward their own personal capabilities to deal with information should be apparent (Bloom, 1976, p. 149). Within the framework of our approach, this sort of attitude will develop only if students have already experienced pleasant emotions during learning.

Development of Attitudes

If we accept the definition of an attitude as an "internal disposition of an organism that affects the choice of objects or personal actions," we can conceive of different ways of facilitating their acquisition. For

---

[9] See Skinner's classic work, *Science and Human Behavior* (1956).

instance, we can use the direct method, modeling, and discussion (Gagné, 1984). In each of these three cases, positive or negative attitudes toward certain tasks, situations, or objects develop within the individual as he or she experiences pleasant or unpleasant emotions in each condition. It should be noted that the methods of instruction described in the paragraphs below are only a beginning. The discussion of method will be expanded in Chapter 6 and amplified in Appendix A.

Direct method. In this case, it is important to directly reward the desired behaviors to ensure that they bring about pleasant emotions. By experiencing pleasant emotions during the accomplishment of a task, the individual develops positive attitudes toward that task. But, in order that there be a pleasant emotion, it is important that the person eventually arrive at the satisfaction of personal needs, often accomplished through some sort of reward, or at least experience the anticipation of need satisfaction. If we hope to help the learner acquire attitudes by a direct method, it is necessary to first identify the person's needs, or, more simply, to identify possible ways of gratifying these needs. This direct method for the acquisition of attitudes can be applied within the framework of training sessions, lessons, courses, or training programs; but above all, in the work setting.

Modeling. Here we are concerned with learning by imitation. In the first place, we must identify one or more models, heroes, or idols of the participant, such as a recognized athlete, political leader, influential student, etc. Next, we must show this model during the performance of a desired behavior, while experiencing pleasant emotions resulting from the targeted behavior. In such cases, it has been demonstrated that the participant will likely choose to act like the model.

Discussion. In this case, the learner is led to see the importance of adopting certain behaviors. We can use the method of role playing and discussion. In the first place, we have the participants play certain roles. They then experience pleasant or unpleasant emotions, which bring about positive or negative attitudes toward the behavior in question.

It is also possible to conduct discussions on selected themes, such as the insidious effects of racial segregation, the advantages and disadvantages of organized sporting activities for children, or ways of improving interpersonal communication. In each of these discussions, the acquisition of positive or negative attitudes can be explained by the fact that the participants experience, through participation, pleasant or unpleasant emotions.

In order that the derived competencies are actually obtained and persist over time, the use of these competencies must provide gratification of the person's needs. We will see how the techniques of reinforcement, modeling, role playing, and discussion can be used to advantage during and after instruction.

During Instruction. From the beginning, for each new course to be developed, the trainer must reflect not only upon the way of helping the learner attain the cognitive objectives, but also upon the means of attaining the affective objectives (attitudes).

During instructional activities, the competencies taught must be reinforced each time that they are adequately used by the learner. Generally, the positive feedback received by the participants during their successful completion of proposed activities will bring about the gratification of needs. For example, during a case study, when participants are asked to present the results of their group work, as the trainer and other participants show their approval for the best work, pleasant emotions will be felt by members of the group presenting their work, and positive attitudes toward these competencies will be developed. The trainer needs to exercise care to ensure that praise is somewhat evenly distributed among the groups, recognizing that undue positive attention to one group can be interpreted as a form of subtle negative feedback to others.

The selection of trainers who can serve as models to the participants is an important application of the principle of modeling. These trainers must be experts in the subject matter in order that their influence as role models can be truly felt.

To sum up this brief discussion of acquisition of positive attitudes during learning, we would say that the following actions are needed:

—**Reinforce the behaviors that are expected to be learned.**
—**Use models (beginning with the trainer).**
—**Use role playing and discussion.**

After Instruction. The first question to address during the design of instructional activities should be to ask if the competencies that learners are supposed to master will be reinforced once their instruction has been completed. Positive attitudes toward these competencies will seldom persist if the person's everyday environment does not allow or reward the use of these competencies. In accomplishing a given task, the employee must see some profit in it. The person must realize that the accomplishment of this task will bring about, in the short term or over time, some combination of personal recognition, self-satisfaction, a bettering of living conditions, etc. The finding that an instructional project has failed can frequently be traced to an absence of any gratification in the work setting.

To sum up this discussion of environmental factors favoring the persistence of positive attitudes, it is essential to:

—Organize the person's work environment or living conditions in such a way that the attitudes acquired during instruction are maintained or enhanced.

This step can be accomplished by: (a) identifying possible rewards (promotions, raises, etc.); (b) designing and implementing a system of rewards; and (c) evaluating and correcting the system as needed.

—Choose participants who can serve as models.

In effect, if the selected participants can act as models for other workers, the attitudes acquired will be much more easily transmitted.

Summary

The design and presentation of instructional activities require more than a knowledge of the learner's progress in cognitive activities. An adequate understanding of the affective component of the person is also necessary.

An understanding of the affective domain presupposes a knowledge of concepts such as needs, expectations, emotions, values, attitudes, and motivation. It also requires some understanding of the interrelationships among these concepts.

Needs of the individual are the source of most actions. Expectations are the mental representations of situations capable of satisfying these needs. We spend a good part of our existence in designing chains of expectations, the actualization of which bring about the satisfaction of our fundamental needs.

To live in balance within the environment, a human being continually compares present reality with personal desires or expectations. When there is a gap between the two, the physiological system is activated. This activation is followed by a cognitive evaluation made by the individual. Generally, a pleasant or unpleasant emotion results from this positive or negative evaluation.

When, during the course of accomplishing a task or interacting with an object or situation, an individual experiences pleasant or unpleasant emotions, the person develops a positive or negative attitude toward these objects, tasks, or situations.

To bridge the gap between an existing situation and expectations, the individual engages in planning. Personal values influence the choice of actions during the formulation of plans.

Motivation can be defined as the effort that the individual is ready to put forth to satisfy personal needs or to experience the pleasant emotions associated with the satisfaction of those needs. Motivation is a function of the intensity of the individual's needs, the size of the task to be accomplished, and the level of success attained during previous accomplishment of similar tasks, and the likelihood of success in this particular situation.

The affective component plays the same dynamic role in learning as it does in everyday life; we actively choose to participate in activities that bring us satisfaction.

Learning permits the acquisition of competencies. Competencies allow the accomplishment of everyday tasks. The accomplishment of tasks allows the realization of intermediate expectations which, in turn, allows the realization of primary expectations. The realization of primary expectations allows for the satisfaction of needs.

Motivation of the learner is thus a function of at least three important factors: the intensity of needs, the perceived size of the learning task, and the attitude held toward the task. It is important to optimize these factors during instruction, and to keep them in mind in the following chapters that consider the cognitive aspects of instruction.

Questions: Chapter 2

For Review:

(1)   Try to suggest one or more need(s) that the following persons are trying to satisfy: (a) John and Betty have been driving for one hour on Highway 50 to find a restaurant; (b) Peter is shopping to buy a necklace for Sue, his girlfriend; (c) Mary enjoys painting; she is working now on what she considers to be the masterpiece of her life; (d) Paul and Joan are very proud of their son; they are borrowing money to give him an excellent education.

(2)   What is the difference between a need and an expectancy?

(3)   Identify a positive or negative emotion you felt recently; (a) describe your expectancy(ies) at the moment the emotion emerged; (b) describe how you viewed the existing situation at that moment; and (c) describe the cognitive evaluation you made when this emotion was felt.

(4)   Suggest three instructional techniques by which the attitudes of an individual may be influenced during instruction. What action might be done after instruction to help maintain or strengthen those attitudes?

(5)   List some positive and negative emotions a learner may feel while engaged in learning. Suggest some ways to enhance or, if necessary, to diminish such emotions.

(6)   Define: (a) motivation; (b) motivation to learn.

(7)   What factors influence the degree of motivation of a person? Try to suggest ways of optimizing these factors with learners.

For Reflection:

(1) How would you explain that, in order to satisfy their needs, some people don't mind cheating, and others do.

(2) Can you think of times when a negative emotion during learning would be desirable from the point of view of the teacher? If you feel that such times do exist, e.g., embarrassment at coming to class unprepared, etc., how should the teacher ensure that such feelings do not generalize to a negative evaluation of the subject matter? Is that result entirely within the control of the teacher?

Chapter 3

Knowledge Representation

If I have an image of what you are, and if you have one of what I am, it is clear that we do not see ourselves as we really are.

Jiddu Krishnamurti, *Freedom from the Known*, **1975**

Introduction

According to Herbert Simon, an organism living in balance with its environment must continually compare its existing situation with a desired situation and then bridge the gap, if one exists, between the two situations. For the two situations to be compared, they must first be represented, in one fashion or another, by the organism making the comparison. In this chapter we will first concern ourselves with the ways that information can be represented in human memory by means of cognitive units[1] called schemas.[2] We will examine in turn different types of knowledge used by the human information processing system during the accomplishment of a complex task. As we examine these various knowledge types, we will provide suggestions for the instructional designer and trainer in structuring the contents of instructional activities.

---

[1] The expression "cognitive unit" is used by J. R. Anderson (1983). Here it refers to concepts, propositions, schemas, etc., all dealt with in the pages which follow.

[2] a. In English, there are two conventions for the plural form of "schema": "schemata" and more recently "schemas." This book will use the simpler form for the plural, i.e., schemas.

   b. In carrying out this work, researchers in artificial intelligence use a variety of means to represent knowledge. We should note, for example, the use of semantic networks, formal logic, rules of production, and utilization of schemas (Anderson, 1984; Harmon & King, 1985). For teaching purposes, we will concern ourselves in this book with the use of schemas as tools for representation.

Theoretical Foundations

The Concept of Schema [3]

Present theories of how humans represent reality have evolved considerably since Plato's almost photographic memory model. Certain models called "constructivist" have been developed, suggesting that external stimuli are not "copies" in memory, but rather are interpreted as a function of the knowledge already possessed by the individual. It is upon this base that several cognitive scientists have built their models of knowledge representation. We will concern ourselves here with the use of schemas as tools for the representation of knowledge. Several simple observations will help us to introduce this concept.

Certainly, at one time or another, you have parked your car in a shopping mall parking lot and then been unable to find it after making your purchases (a frustration!). Your forgetting can be explained as an instance of your neglecting to formulate any explicit prescriptions relative to this particular place at the time you parked your car (for example: "My car is in front of the neon sign," or "My car is near the second lamp post"). In other words, as you parked the car, you neglected to activate encoding procedures,[4] and since you had used no coding scheme, you had no benchmarks to consult for the needed information. But what does this process of encoding pertinent information resemble, and, more specifically, what are the memory structures capable of being used during encoding?

To simplify matters, we can suppose that a human being has in memory a vast repertoire of generalized propositions of the type "X is in front of Y," "X is near Y," etc. At the time that we are encoding, we activate these generalized propositions and assign certain values to the variables contained in the propositions. In this way we build specific propositions of the type: "My car is in front of the neon sign," or "My car is near the second lamp post." These generic knowledge structures carry the name of *schemas.* Cognitive scientists generally reserve the term *schema* for substantial cognitive entities. In this text, the pattern set by

---

[3]   See also Brien, 1983.

[4]   According to Tulving, encoding "is the process that transforms an event or a fact into a memory trace."

Rumelhart and Ortony (1977), *we will consider a schema to designate all cognitive structures composed of relations and/or operations and variables.* For these authors, schemas exist to allow the representation of knowledge relative to objects, situations, events, sequences of events, actions, and sequences of actions. This perspective is also that adopted by Ausubel (1968). Here is another example of a schema:

Imagine that a friend says, "I had breakfast at McDonalds this morning." How could it be that, without your ever visiting the location he or she had in mind, you could ask questions such as: "Did you wait long in line?" or "Did you get good service?" Such a situation is relatively simple to explain within the framework of schema theory. Because you yourself have gone to this type of restaurant a number of times, you also possess a schema of a "Meal at McDonalds."[5] This schema is composed of a given set of general propositions of the type: "X stands in line," "Y serves X," "Z prepares the food," etc.[6] When we tell you that we ate at McDonalds, you activate your own schema. That action is what permits you to understand what we are saying and to ask pertinent questions.

Several interesting exercises have been found to demonstrate the power of schemas to represent knowledge (Anderson, 1984). Some of these cases are relatively simple to reproduce. For example, we can give to a first group of subjects the passage that appears below and then to another group the same passage, but with the title changed (the alternate title is "Interplanetary Voyage to an Inhabited Planet"). The effects of the title change on comprehension are startling.

While watching a parade from the 40th Floor:

What an amazing view! Through the window you can see the crowd below. At this distance, everything appears minuscule, but you can still distinguish the brilliant colors of clothing. Everyone seems to

---

5   Schemas are generally acquired by induction. After having found himself in the same situation or having accomplished a task a certain number of times, a person, using already existing schemas, builds a new schema.

6   It is important to note that your schema of a meal at McDonalds does not necessarily match our schema in every way. This variation is the phenomenon that we make reference to when we say that humans store information in their own idiosyncratic way. But our schemas generally have enough elements in common that we can understand each other.

move forward in order, all moving in the same direction. There are
apparently young children as well as adults.

(Lindsay & Norman, 1977)

We then ask the subjects of the two groups to read the passage in
silence. After reading it, we ask all of them to summarize the material
they have just read. It is always interesting to note that, having read
identical texts (except the title), the subjects of the two groups provide
different versions of what they have read. Those in the first group
describe a parade, when the others describe an interplanetary voyage. We
can explain this phenomenon by supposing that, while the subjects read
the title, they activate one or more schemas related to a parade or to an
interplanetary voyage depending upon their particular group assignment.

Anatomy of a Schema

The concept of schema can be explained by means of relationships
taken from modern logic, the most significant of which are works of
Boole and DeMorgan (Cofi, 1972). In logic, a relationship describes a
linkage between two or more variables. One can say, for example, that
the proposition "A is larger than B" (where "A" and "B" are variables
and "larger than," a relationship) expresses a linkage between the
variables A and B. By giving different values to a relationship of this
type, one can build an infinite number of specific propositions, such as
"10 is larger than 5" or "100 is larger than 99." Moreover, such
relationships are not limited just to numbers. Let's consider, for example,
two persons, A and B, where A represents the mother and B her child. In
this case, the subject who already has in memory the mother-child
relationship can say that "Dorothy is Christi's mother." Having acquired
such a relationship, a person can represent for himself or herself and can
comprehend a portion of reality.

We can also use a relationship to represent certain phenomena dealing
with more than two variables. Thus, a statement such as "David gives the
ball to John" can be stored in memory through the mediation of a schema
of the type "an actor gives an object to a receiver." This schema thereby
allows the formulation of particular propositions such as "David gives
the ball to John." Researchers in cognitive science realized early the

power of the relational concept; in fact, certain authors made it the basis of their system of knowledge representation.

A schema can be represented by the following symbolic notion: R (V_1, V_2, ... V_n) where V_1, V_2, ... V_n represent variables or arguments and R expresses the type of relationship existing among variables or arguments. Thus, we could represent the schema cited above as: "Give (actor, object, receiver)," which is read as "(an) actor gives an object to a receiver." Once this general schema has been instantiated, we have a particular proposition "give (David, ball, John)." We need to emphasize here that one can assign to the variables not only "particular" values, but also "general" values, as we do in algebra when a variable is replaced by an expression itself containing variables. For example, we could replace the variables in our hypothetical schema, "give (actor, object, receiver)," with the values "rich," "money," and "poor" to obtain the proposition "give (rich, money, poor)" which, we can see, is a general schema or proposition worth investigating.

Role of Schemas in Everyday Life

Schemas can be seen as *generic knowledge structures which permit human beings to represent reality and to act upon it.* When it comes to representing objects or events, we say that the person is using *declarative* schemas. On the other hand, if the task at hand requires the execution of a physical or intellectual operation, we say that the person is using a *procedural* schema. In the paragraphs below, particular attention is paid to the role schemas play in the comprehension and retrieval of information. Next, we examine the different types of knowledge most frequently encountered in teaching and instruction, explaining the schemas most useful in representing them. A similar examination allows us to formulate suggestions to assist the designer and the teacher in their work in structuring the content of learning activities.

Schemas and Comprehension of Reality

In an interesting article, Rumelhart (1980) presents schemas as "the building blocks of cognition." According to him, a schema such as "give (actor, object, receiver)" allows comprehension of all events of the type

"David gives the ball to John," "Mary gives the apple to Paul," i.e., events possessing this same structure. Given a particular event, action is first detected by the observer, who then draws upon a schema already present in memory, which then becomes usable to represent the observed fact.[7] If this search in memory is fruitful, the values "David," "ball," and "John" are then assigned to the schema's variables, and, in the case of a match between the recalled schema and the observed event, comprehension occurs.

We can suppose that, in some cases, when the particular concepts are assigned to the variables of a schema, a mental image is produced (Denis, 1989). This line of reasoning has been used in sports, where visual imaging has been shown to improve performance (e.g., Gallway, 1984).

Schemas and Information Recall

The schemas already present in memory act as mediators for the recall of past events. Thus, if a person is faced with a fact tied to an event in the past, the schema that previously served to encode the event is now recalled and used to reconstruct the event. If, during the process of recall, the values of certain variables are not assigned, the system compensates by using "default values," i.e., plausible ones based upon prior experience (Rumelhart & Ortony, 1977). For example, taking the schema of a restaurant, someone questioning an informant could deduce that the person stood in line a long time, if the person reports that the visit occurred on a particular day of the week (Saturday or Sunday, for example) is mentioned. Thus, we see that humans constantly make inferences in their thinking about everyday events by inserting details they cannot possibly know for certain. The phenomenon of using schemas to recall past events explains the "reconstructive" nature of human memory (Rumelhart & McClelland, 1986).

---

[7] See Hoc (1988) for a more detailed explanation as to the ways in which schemas are activated.

Different Kinds of Knowledge

One of the principal tasks of an instructional designer is the structuring of lesson, course, and program content.[8] If we hope to facilitate learning, we must keep in mind the assimilating role of schemas. There are, of course, other principles to observe during the design of instructional activities, but the assimilating role of schemas is fundamental (see Ausubel, 1968). Before examining the different kinds of knowledge that the designer or trainer frequently encounters, we should briefly distinguish the concepts of: (1) information coming from context, (2) classifying schemas, and (3) knowledge.

Whenever an individual interacts with an environment, he or she receives information holistically from the environment. The person first has to assimilate the information into an existing set of schemas and, from this process of assimilation will emerge the individual's personal knowledge relative to this environment. In the process of acquiring knowledge, the information coming from the environment serves as input, and the schemas of the individual are the structures used for encoding this information, resulting in knowledge as output. From examining this process, we can understand that two different observers receiving input from the same environment can acquire different understandings if they use different receiving schemas. The quotation from Krishnamurti at the beginning of this chapter illustrates this phenomenon.

If the structuring of the content of instructional activities consists in determining the order of presentation of different knowledge elements, then the classifying of different types of knowledge into major categories is important. The authors of taxonomies such as Bloom (1956), Gagné (1984), and Merrill (1987) have applied themselves to this task. Instead of offering an exhaustive list, we suggest below certain types of knowledge most commonly encountered in an educational context. In doing so, we will suggest a structure of schemas that can facilitate the

---

[8] For the time being, we will define the content of training activities as the set of knowledge that participants must acquire. Structuring the content of training activities, where these are enabled by written text, spoken word, or pictorially, consists of organizing the knowledge to present in such a way as to facilitate assimilation by the learner.

assimilation of such knowledge and will propose the means for guiding the designer in structuring the content of instructional activities.

Concepts

The idea that a schema expresses a relationship among variables was described earlier, as was the notion that a schema is transformed into a particular (or general) proposition when certain values are assigned to its variables. Concepts can be likened to values, general or particular, attributed to the variables of a schema to form a new proposition. Thus, in the statement, "John gives an apple to Mary," "John," "apple," and "Mary" are the concepts, particular in this case, which have been assigned to the variables of a schema of the type: "give (actor, object, receiver)" to make a particular proposition. In the same way, general concepts like "rich," "money," and "poor" could have been assigned to the same schema to form a general proposition of the type "The rich give their money to the poor," as we saw on the preceding pages. Thus, we see that the notion of a concept has a very specific meaning in Norman and Rumelhart's model. In their view, concepts are cognitive units used for representing particular objects or actions (John, a particular action executed by him, a specific ball) or classes of objects or of actions (rich, money, poor, and the general action of giving).

For these researchers, the representation of a new concept presupposes that the learner already possesses information of three types: (1) the class to which the object being represented belongs; (2) one or more differentiating characteristics of this object or action; and (3) one or more examples of this object or action (Lindsay & Norman, 1977). Thus, for example, the representation of the concept "rectangle,"[9] is done by means of an emerging concept of the class of "four-sided figures" (formally, "quadrilaterals"). It is clarified by knowing the characteristics of a rectangle and by being exposed to examples of squares, rectangles, and irregular figures like trapezoids. Eventually, the person comes to recognize the class ("four-sided figures"), distinguish these different four-sided figures, and can consistently identify and eventually produce a rectangle.

---

[9]   To simplify matters, we define the rectangle as "a quadrilateral with right angles and opposite sides parallel."

We can then posit that the acquisition of a new concept by the learner will be facilitated (a) if one helps the learner link this concept to be learned with a more general concept already known (e.g., if one attempts to help the learner connect the concept of "rectangle" with that of a "quadrilateral"); (b) if the learner possesses the prerequisite concepts, in this case the particular characteristics of the new concept (right angles, parallel sides); and (c) if we furnish the learner with examples of the new concept (pictures of different rectangles). In other words, the acquisition of a new concept will be helped if the learner already possesses a schema in the form given below and if the person takes care to assign appropriate values to the variables involved:

is-a (x, y)

and

has $(x, c^1, c^2, c^3, ... c^n)$

(where **x** is the concept to define, **y** is the class, c^1, c^2, c^3 c^n ..., are the characteristics; **is-a**, **and**, **has** are the relations)

Thus, we can draw together the key ideas from the preceding lines with the following prescription regarding teaching concepts:

To enhance the encoding of a new concept, the trainer should, as a minimum: (1) check to see that the learner has an appropriate schema for coding the concept;[10] (2) make sure, as the instruction begins, that the learner possesses a more abstract, but related concept (i.e., a class of objects to which the new concept belongs), as well as the characteristics of the concept to acquire; and (3) provide the learner with examples of the new concept.

---

[10] This sort of schema is normally acquired during childhood.

Propositions

In our comprehension of reality, concepts are rarely used in an isolated fashion. Most of the time, they appear in combination, permitting the person to represent a portion of reality.

As we have seen previously, a schema contains a relationship and a certain number of variables, as the example below illustrates:

give (actor, object, receiver)

Within this frame of reference, a given sentence could refer to several propositional schemas.[11] For example, in physics, Newton's Law, or the law of universal gravitation, can be stated as follows: "Two material objects each exert an attraction on the other that varies directly with their mass and inversely with the square of the distance separating them." This proposition draws upon at least two key schemas: that of "proportional relationships" and that of "inverse relationships," which the student must first possess in order to understand Newton's Law. Thus, in the structuring of activities for instruction, one must identify as accurately as possible the key schemas before proceeding with the structuring of course content.

In order to arrive at comprehension or to gain an internal representation of a new proposition, the learner must possess an appropriate receiving schema and the concepts likely to be assigned to the variables of this schema. Thus, we can formulate the following statement relative to the acquisition of propositions:

---

[11] This is an appropriate place to stress the fundamental differences that linguists make between **surface structure** and **deep structure**. In the case of surface structure, we refer to the words and the syntax (their relations including grammar) of discourse; in deep structure, we refer to the ideas referred to by words. The schemas, concepts, propositions, and other cognitive units referred to in the pages which follow make up deep structure. During the structuring of content for training activities, we must concern ourselves not just with the sentences themselves, but also with their referents—the objects or ideas referred to. In a course, there may only be some key concepts and other cognitive units upon which hang all other elements of the course. It is these key cognitive units that should attract the attention of the designer and the trainer, since they form the basis for all expected learning.

To facilitate the encoding by the learner of a new proposition, one must: (1) be sure that the learner possesses, as a beginning, the concepts required in the proposition; and (2) activate an appropriate receiving schema.

Thus, in the example given above, if one wishes to ensure that the learner comprehends Newton's Law, he or she must begin with a grasp of the schemas for "proportional relationship" and for "inverse relationship." The learner must also possess the concepts of "attractive force" and of "mass," as well as "distance" and "square."

Before proceeding further with our study of different types of knowledge, it is necessary to stress the fundamental role played by propositions in knowledge representation. Propositions constitute the primary element of knowledge to be acquired (Anderson, 1981; Ellen Gagné, 1985). We can compare the role played by propositions in the makeup of other knowledge to that of the atom in the composition of various molecules that make up matter.

Episodes

Concepts and propositions by themselves are not enough to represent reality. These elements of knowledge are habitually grouped into combinations that we call episodes.[12] Thus, the verbal description that one gives of a dinner at a restaurant, or that of a trip by plane, can only bring out the appropriate episodes in the mind of the listener, *if the person possesses the appropriate receiving schema.* These episodes consist of propositions, which are themselves composed of concepts. To understand the description of a trip someone has made by airplane, the assimilator schema could have the following form:

Reserve (individual, ticket)

and

---

[12] We will consider principles, laws, and processes as belonging to the category of episodes.

arrive (individual, airport)

and

check (individual, baggage)

and

obtain (individual, boarding pass)

and

pass (individual, security gate)

etc.

The analysis of this schema informs us of the necessary elements for comprehending an episode. First, comprehension will be facilitated if the learner possesses an appropriate assimilator schema.[13] In addition, so that the episode is understood, certain propositions must be constructed, and, for this construction to take place, the appropriate schemas must be made part of the repertoire of the learner. The concepts assigned to schemas must be in the repertoire of the learner. We can sum up the previous ideas with the following proposition:

> *To help in the encoding of an episode, it is necessary to: (a) be sure that the learner possesses the concepts and propositions that make up the episode; and (b) activate an appropriate receptor schema.*

---

[13]   Most of the time in teaching, we use analogies or metaphors to activate appropriate assimilator schemas. Thus, to help someone understand the cycle of water in nature, we compare it to the process of water evaporating in a kettle, followed by the condensation of drops on the ceiling. In this regard, the reflections of Gentner & Gentner (1983) make interesting reading (see also Howard, 1987, and West, Farmer, & Wolff, 1991).

Production Rules

An adaptive organism does not just represent objects or events. Most of the time, it must act on reality in a way to bridge the gap between an existing situation and its expectations. To bring about these transformations, the organism's information processing system uses procedural knowledge, for which the production rules are quite simple. These consist of propositions of the type: "If a certain condition is met" then "take this action" or "carry out this operation." We can represent these production rules symbolically as follows:

if condition x

then action y

Within the context that interests us, production rules can be built in the following manner: "If I wish to transform an initial situation $S_{(i)}$ to a situation $S_{(i + 1)}$, then I must utilize operation y." In most cases, production rules[14] are constituted from several conditions, as in the example of a hypothetical expert system[15] as proposed by Gallaire (1985):

---

[14] We can consider production rules as cognitive units used to transform a given state into another state or to associate a given state with another state.

[15] An expert system is a computerized system that imitates a human expert in resolving problems. In recent years expert systems have become the object of intensive research in artificial intelligence. These systems are used in different knowledge domains such as geology, education, and medicine. In medicine, expert systems are used to help the doctor or other health professional in the diagnosis of illness. By giving the system a certain amount of data about the patient, the system "deduces," by means of production rules it possesses, the particular illnesses. See Harmon & King (1985) for an introduction to expert systems, and see McFarland & Parker (1990) for an explanation of the applicability of such systems in education and training environments.

R1: If the patient has a skin rash and has:
           low fever
           enlarged lymph nodes on back of head
           no pustules
           no congestion
    Then: diagnose as rubella (German measles)

R2: If isolated sores
           itching
           low fever
           pustules or vesicles (blisters)
           scabbing occurs quickly
    Then: diagnose as varicella (chicken pox)

R3: If congestion is evident
           hurting eyes (eyes sensitive to light)
           red spots on skin
           high fever
    Then: diagnose as rubeola (red measles)

R4: If tonsils are red
           desquamation (skin sloughing)
           high fever
           bright red spots on skin
    Then: diagnose as scarlatina (scarlet fever).

From this analysis it is apparent that one or more conditions of a production rule are made up of propositions which, by themselves, contain concepts. Production rules consist also, in the action part, of operations to execute. If we want to teach a certain rule, ideally the learner must understand the propositions that make it up (which presupposes that he or she possesses the appropriate schemas and concepts) and can execute the pertinent operations. We emphasize here, once again, the importance of the learner having mastered the appropriate prerequisites. That consideration leads us to suggest the following:

*To facilitate the encoding of a production rule, one must
(1) be certain that the learner possesses the concepts,*

***propositions, and operations required by that production
rule; and (2) activate the appropriate receptor schema.***

For the medical example cited above, diagnosing certain infectious
diseases, there were certain necessary concepts, propositions, and
schemas. The trainer would first make sure that the learner understands
concepts (like dizziness, pustules, congestion), as well as the propositions
(the condition or first part of the rule), and operations (the second part of
the rule), and then the appropriate receptor schema (the if-then schema).

Procedures

Often, in accomplishing a task, it is a set of production rules that the
information processing system uses. We give the name of *procedure* or
algorithm to these sets of production rules (Landa, 1983). Here again, the
possession of appropriate receptor schemas facilitates learning. To teach
the procedure for solving linear equations, we can compare the equation
to a balance-scale in equilibrium and the appropriate rules of transformation to actions taken to keep the balance in equilibrium (additions of the
same quantity to each side of the balance, taking away the same quantity
from each side, etc.). In most cases, the procedures consist of sub-
procedures as illustrated in the diagram of Figure 5.

Figure 5. Breakdown of a procedure into its sub-procedures.
(Changing gears with a standard transmission)

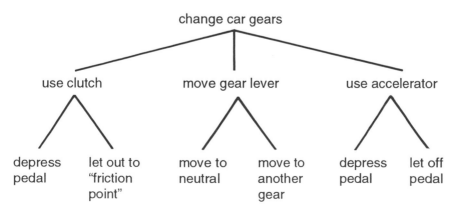

In order for **procedure a** to be executed, it is necessary that **procedures b and c** be executable, and for these last two to execute, **procedures d and e, as well as f and g** are required. The execution of complex procedures, as in the calculation of the variance or the standard deviation in statistics, presupposes the execution of sub-procedures such as the calculation of the mean. The calculation of the mean presupposes, in turn, the presence of sub-procedures such as addition and division of numbers. It is the absence of such prerequisite skills that causes many of the failures in mathematics.

Heuristics

If we consider the program conceived by a computer programmer as a procedure, which of the elements of that person's previous knowledge guided him in the search for an adequate sequence of operations for the program? We generally reserve the term "heuristic" for production rules which guide the steps of someone looking for a problem solution. Heuristics are rules used for managing information, and that is why we consider them to be at a superior level to the entities discussed above. These production rules are used during the planning of procedures or, in general, in the search for the solution to problems.[16] For example, in the hypothetical expert system suggested by Gallaire and referred to above, in order for the system to select the appropriate production rules, "meta-rules" (MR's) or heuristics are needed. For example, the following meta-rules are suggested:

MR(1)   **If there are lesions or a rash,**
              Then diagnose R(1), R(2), R(3), R(4).

---

[16] Simon (1981b) describes well what is meant by the term heuristic: "... human reasoning, the aptitude for resolving problems, from the most maladroit to the most capable, does nothing more than to put to work various mixes of trial and error or of selectivity. Selectivity itself follows from diverse empirical rules, or heuristics, which suggest certain itineraries to try first and those which can be promising." See also the work of Anderson (1985) for an interesting overview of strategies for problem solving.

MR(2)   **If the patient is an adult woman
and if R(1), R(2), R(3), or R(4) are
diagnosed,
R(1) has priority.**

As we can see from comparing these production rules (of the heuristic type) with those cited earlier, heuristics act upon production rules which, in turn, act directly on the representation of objects or facts. In this context, it is possible to apply the suggestion formulated earlier for encoding production rules to the teaching of heuristics. But it should be understood that, in this case, teaching presupposes the mastery of a considerable number of other cognitive units, such as concepts, propositions, episodes, and production rules, because heuristics are acquired during the repeated manipulation of such cognitive units.

Blocks of Knowledge: "Chunking"

Up until now in the discussion, we have dealt only with the acquisition of relatively constrained cognitive units, what Farreny (1985) has termed "granules of knowledge." The content of instructional activities always requires the acquisition of considerable quantities of knowledge. It is therefore necessary to give particular attention to the organization of knowledge in memory if it is to be recalled and transferred at the right moment. Most research shows that regardless of when it is structured, information is better understood and is retrieved more easily if organized by the designer, before the presentation of information, or by the learner, at the actual moment of learning (Ausubel, 1968).

Normally, the limited capacity of short-term memory[17] will not inhibit the acquisition of a relatively limited amount of knowledge. Generally, this capacity is sufficient if, as suggested by Anderson (1981), the

---

[17] While the present text does not expand upon the concepts of short-term and long-term memory, it is possible to define them briefly here. Long-term memory is the set of cognitive units that an individual possesses. Short-term memory, or "working memory" is considered as the areas where mental operations are executed and where the results of mental operations are temporarily stored. For an excellent discussion of the differences between long-term and short-term memory, see Ormrod (1989).

comprehension of an event does not require that a comparison be made with a schema just activated in short-term memory. The process of comprehension is always complicated when the content to be taught requires blocks of information, as is generally the case in scholarly subjects. It is highly probable, in these cases, that the limits of short-term memory will be an obstacle to the acquisition and retrieval of information. This problem can be avoided if one takes care to *organize* these blocks of knowledge before communicating them.

Thus, as Reigeluth, Merrill, Wilson, and Spiller (1980) have proposed and as West, Farmer, and Wolff (1991) have elaborated upon, different kinds of larger structures or "macro-schemas" can facilitate the acquisition of large sets of knowledge (see also Berlyne, 1965, and Ausubel, 1968). As an example, one could structure a course in auto mechanics in such a way as to present first the different sub-systems of an automobile and then explain in detail the mechanical devices which make up each of them. For example, once the function of the engine cooling system is understood, the specific parts, such as the exhaust manifold, radiator, and water pump, are more easily understood. In this case, we can say that we use a structure of the type "taxonomy of parts." In other circumstances, the content can be organized with the help of a structure of the type "taxonomy of species," as in the classification of animals into categories and subcategories. In this context, the acquisition of a large quantity of knowledge can be facilitated by the presence in memory of macro-schemas. We can thus formulate the following suggestion:

> *To facilitate the encoding of large chunks of knowledge, one must activate the appropriate macro-schemas.*

Importance of Prior Knowledge

During this chapter the reader will most likely have noted the major role played by pre-existing knowledge in instruction. In order for competencies to be acquired, it is essential that the learner bring to the task the important elements of knowledge required by the task. These elements of knowledge consist of concepts, propositions, episodes, production rules, procedures, or heuristics. These diverse cognitive units, as noted earlier, are interrelated. New concepts are built upon the foundation of older ones, and new propositions are formed with concepts already possessed by the learner. The same goes for the other cognitive units, without mentioning the key role in assimilation played by schemas during encoding of these diverse knowledge structures. Figure 6 shows the ties between these diverse cognitive units.

Figure 6. Ties between diverse cognitive units.

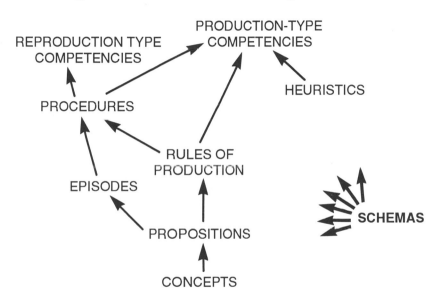

The relationships between the diverse cognitive units examined in this chapter may lead us to think of instruction as being necessarily linear. In Chapter 5 we will see that a diversity of instructional methods can be used, depending upon whether a direct or an indirect teaching approach is preferred.[18]

---

[18] In a direct approach to instruction, the ties to prior knowledge are explicitly taken into account, while in an indirect approach, the learner acquires the prior knowledge through guided discovery.

Know-that and Know-how

This brief overview of the different types of knowledge puts in relief an interesting problem raised by cognitive scientists, i.e., how to know if the various elements of knowledge utilized in information processing are declarative or procedural (Anderson, 1983). In the context of cognitive sciences, we generally say that declarative knowledge is used to represent objects and events, while procedural knowledge is used to represent operations to execute upon the objects or from a given set of events. In the context of instruction, we say that declarative knowledge is the "know(ing)-that," while procedural knowledge is what we call "know-how."

To illustrate this problem, let us draw upon the analysis of Daniel Berlyne (1965), for whom reasoning consists in transforming a given situation S_i (represented internally by a *situational thought*) by means of operators O_i (represented internally by a *transformational thought*), in a manner to change S_i to S_{i+1}. In this way, Berlyne then arrives at proposing the concept of chains of thoughts (S_i--O_i--S_{i+1}---O_{i+1}, etc.) that one could consider as one's "tracks" through the process of thought.

Within this frame of reference, we can consider *situational thoughts* as declarative knowledge that permits the person to represent objects and events for himself, and *transformational thoughts* as procedural knowledge which permits him to act on these objects and events. Thus, the notion of concepts, propositions, and episodes examined previously can be considered as declarative knowledge that makes up *situational thoughts*; and production rules, procedures, and heuristics can be considered as procedure knowledge or *transformational thoughts*.

But this way of seeing does not completely inform us of the declarative or procedural nature of our knowledge, because of the possibility of representing *transformational thoughts* through the means of declarative knowledge. This is what is demonstrated by the fact that an individual can describe the production rules, procedures, and heuristics without being able to apply them (Hoc, 1988). From these reflections, an acceptable working hypothesis can be derived. A portion of our knowledge would be declarative and another part procedural, depending upon the task to accomplish. Thus, when the task is to *describe* objects, events, and procedures, one can say that we use declarative knowledge for representing the contents of memory to communicate. In addition, when the task requires *acting upon reality*, we use declarative knowledge to represent different situations and procedural knowledge to transform these situations. But, in every case, we must emphasize that our declarative or procedural knowledge is held in memory in propositional form. It is only when procedural knowledge is activated that the operations attached to it are activated.

For example, if someone teaches a new driver to drive with an automatic transmission, the person receives verbal instruction as to how to move the gear lever (D for driving forward or R to go backward—but from a parked position). The information is given and received as declarative knowledge. If the person never sits at the steering wheel, but instead simply talks about it, it remains declarative knowledge. However, if the person sits in the driver's seat and practices moving the gear lever, mentally or physically, it quickly becomes procedural knowledge (i.e., know-how). After using this procedure frequently enough for it to become automatic, it has become almost entirely procedural. In order for our now more experienced driver to describe to another person exactly what to do, it becomes necessary to concentrate and retrieve the previously learned declarative knowledge.

To sum up, we can consider an individual's cognitive structure as consisting of two sets of knowledge: one set made up of declarative knowledge (what one knows, set A in Figure 7) and a second set consisting of procedural knowledge (one's know-how, set B in the illustration). But, as is illustrated in Figure 7, the distinction is not always so clear-cut between declarative and procedural knowledge. In fact, there is frequently an overlap of the two sets. As an example, anyone in a teaching or training position must necessarily possess both types of knowledge in being able to accomplish the task and verbally explain the procedure.

The degree of overlap helps emphasize the fact that an individual can possess knowledge that is declarative and procedural at the same time, a kind of "dual knowledge" (George, 1983). This type of knowledge is what is required of the teacher to explain the procedures of a given domain and also to execute them. In addition, the reader should note that in this text, we have been careful to specify that set B is made up of "executable procedures," emphasizing that a person can be capable of executing certain procedures without being able to describe them, just as it is possible to describe certain procedures without being able to carry them out.

Figure 7. Declarative and procedural knowledge and their overlap.

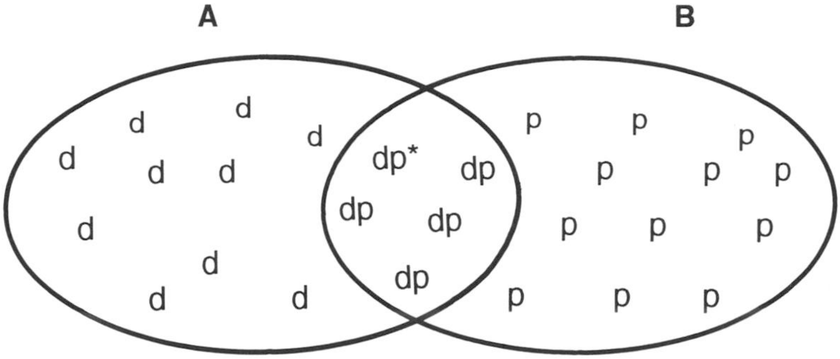

*: the intersection of d & p, having the characteristics of both

Figure 7 also suggests a certain plasticity to our knowledge. According to certain cognitive scientists (notably J. R. Anderson, 1983), knowledge relative to a certain procedure is acquired first in a declarative form, but then later is transformed into an executable procedure. We see this phenomenon frequently in the teaching of certain subject areas such as physics, chemistry, biology, or grammar, when one first proposes to the student the theory and then subsequently brings the person little by little to the practice. We should note that not all of the individual's declarative knowledge will be transformed into procedural knowledge. The definitions, laws, and principles of a discipline will stay in a declarative form, even if they are the basis for an elaboration of procedures. We too frequently have the tendency, in designing instructional activities, to emphasize only the learning of procedures, taking for granted the knowledge from which the procedures were derived. Unfortunately, sooner or later, the learner will eventually be confronted with a problem which can be solved only by a return to the basic concepts of the discipline. In such cases, the underlying declarative knowledge is of vital importance (Hoc, 1988).

Mental Models

To conclude this chapter, it is worth remembering that the accomplishment of a task does not occur in a vacuum, and that expertise requires much more than simply acquiring a few bits of declarative and procedural knowledge. Whenever we take action, we act on a system which is itself a subsystem of some more encompassing system. We mention this fact as a reminder that all of these elements of action are complex.

The representation made by a person of the different states and the diverse transformations that can arise in a given system constitute that person's own mental model of the system in question (Norman, 1983, 1988). This mental model is composed of declarative and procedural knowledge that the person possesses related to the target-system. Thus, the surgeon doing open heart surgery must have the most accurate mental model possible of the functioning of the human heart. With this model, the surgeon can simulate the various heart functions and can take the appropriate action to ensure the success of the operation. Another model of group functioning also allows the team leader of a heart operation to understand the role of each member of the surgical team, assisting them all in the accomplishment of their tasks, in this case performing a heart operation.

Psychologists have long known the key role played by mental models in information processing. Studies in recent years have shown that certain accidents in nuclear power plants could be traced back to human error due to the absence of appropriate mental models on the part of the operators (Norman, 1983). What kind of mental model must an operator of a nuclear reactor have? Does the training of such an operator need to be at the level of an engineer or that of a technician? These are the kinds of questions that interest the cognitive scientist (Rogers, Rutherford, & Bibby, 1992).

For the trainer, the importance of motivating the learner to develop the appropriate mental models does not have to be demonstrated. According to certain authors (Norman, 1983; Gentner & Gentner, 1983; Vosniadou & Ortony, 1989) the role of analogy in instruction is fundamental, because analogies activate the necessary schemas in the mind of the learner to obtain appropriate mental models.

Summary

In order to remain in equilibrium with the environment, a human being continually compares reality with desires. To make such a comparison, the person must represent for himself, in one form or another, both the reality and his expectations. Several means exist for representing this knowledge. In this chapter, we have been particularly interested in the use of schemas.

ᶜSchemas are generic structures of knowledge that permit the human to represent reality for himself and to act upon this representation. They are made up of relations and/or operations and of variables. The individual abstracts schemas using already existing schemas and the repeated observation of objects or events, or by the repeated execution of actions.

When the values are assigned to variables of a schema, it is transformed into general or specific knowledge. Thus, schemas give birth to cognitive units such as concepts, propositions, episodes, production rules, procedures, and heuristics.

Certain rules must be respected during the teaching of these diverse cognitive units. Ideally, if one wishes to facilitate the encoding of a particular cognitive unit, one must activate an appropriate receptor schema. One must also see that the learner possesses the prerequisite cognitive units for the acquisition of the desired knowledge or skill.

We can classify knowledge into two major categories: declarative knowledge (the knowing-that) and procedural knowledge (the know-how). Declarative knowledge is used to represent reality, and procedural knowledge is used to act upon that reality.

When one wishes to acquire a given competency, it is important to concern oneself with the connections between prior knowledge and the present knowledge this competency is built upon.

Mastery of a given content or subject matter requires more than simply the possession of separate bits of declarative and procedural knowledge. Quality learning requires the construction of appropriate mental models in the head of the learner. A mental model consists of a required set of declarative and procedural knowledge permitting the representation of the system upon which the learner can then act.

Questions: Chapter 3

For review:

(1) In order to change a current state into a desired one, an adaptive organism has to be able to represent these states internally. What is the basic cognitive unit that a human being uses to represent these states?

(2) Define the following terms: schema, production rules, procedures, and heuristics.

(3) How does a schema differ from the representation of specific knowledge?

(4) Take a few minutes to read the following text by Bransford and Johnson, 1973 (cited in Howard, 1987), then try to make a summary. Why is it so hard to summarize?

The procedure is actually quite simple. First you arrange things into different groups. Of course, one pile may be sufficient depending on how much there is to do. If you have to go somewhere else due to lack of facilities that is the next step, otherwise you are pretty well set. It is important not to overdo things. That is, it is better to do few things at once than too many. In the short run, this may not seem important but complications can easily arise. A mistake can be expensive as well. At first the whole procedure will seem complicated. Soon, however, it will become just another facet of life. It is difficult to foresee any end to the necessity for this task in the immediate future, but then one can never tell. After the procedure is completed one arranges the materials into different groups again. Then they can be put in their appropriate places. Eventually they will be used once more and the whole cycle will then have to be repeated. However, that is part of life.

(5)   What are the two types of knowledge explained by Anderson (1985)? In what ways does one type impact the other?

(6)   What other cognitive units need to be in the memory of the learner prior to the comprehension of a new production rule? of large chunks of knowledge? of a new schema? of a reproduction-type competency?

For reflection:

(1)   What mechanisms might explain a total change of a person's understanding of specific domain, i.e., a "paradigm shift"?

Chapter 4

Accomplishment of a Complex Task[1]

If one has determined in advance the words to be pronounced, there will be no hesitation. If one has determined in advance one's business, one's occupation in the world, by that alone one will easily advance.

Confucius

---

[1] Here we refer to tasks requiring execution of a large number of operations, the kinds of tasks that one generally encounters in exercising a trade, an art, or a profession. Examples would be the task of a plumber installing a bathroom sink, an accountant filling out a tax return, or an artist painting a canvas.

Introduction

When an adaptive organism determines that an existing situation is at variance with its expectations, it generally conceives of a plan for transforming the situation in the desired direction. In this chapter, we will be most interested in the dynamics of planning and executing an action. In basing our case on the arguments of Luria (1973, 1980), and Fodor (1986) concerning the modular structure of the mind, we will consider the human information processing system as regrouping a set of hierarchical functions for which the underlying procedures are activated during the planning and execution of an action. When the individual perceives a discrepancy between that which exists and personal expectations, he or she then sets out a plan for the accomplishment of a relevant task by means of the brain's planning function. Next, the person calls upon operator, verbal, or motor functions from the cerebral cortex to execute the plan.

In this chapter, these theoretical foundations permit us to construct a step-by-step model for the accomplishment of a task, and in the next chapter to propose a definition of the concept of competency.

Dynamics of the Accomplishment of a Complex Task [2]

We can analyze the process of planning and execution of an action by a human being by observing the functioning of the brain during the accomplishment of operational, verbal, or motor tasks. In the first part of this chapter, we will attempt to construct such a representation. As a beginning, we will briefly examine the principal components of the human brain as described by Luria (1973, 1980) to help us understand some of the functions assumed by these components.

---

[2] See also Brien and Duchastel (1986).

Basic Components of the Human Brain

In his book, *The Working Brain*, the Russian neuropsychologist Aleksandr R. Luria describes three principal components of the human brain (Luria, 1973). The affective component, dealt with in the second chapter of this book, has the function of regulating the level of neuron activity required for the activation of the information processing necessary for the planning and execution of an action. This regulatory function is mainly assured by certain components in the lower part of the brain, the reptilian brain, and particularly by the reticular activation system.

Figure 8. Reticular activation system.

(Arrows show pathways of sensory stimulation)

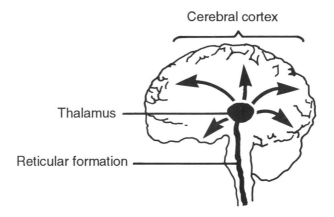

The second component, the perceptual function, requires the perception of external stimuli and their representation and storage in long-term memory. This function seems to be carried out by procedures encoded in the groups of neurons in the occipital lobe, the sensory areas, the parietal lobes, and the left temporal lobe (see Figure 9).

The third component, the action function, is responsible for the programming of action plans and for the verification of adequate execution of the plans. This function seems to be mainly carried out in the frontal lobes of the cerebral cortex.

Figure 9. Selected components of the human brain.

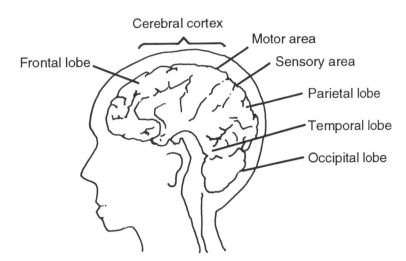

While having specific roles, these components act in complementary fashion (Luria, 1973, p. 99). Thus, it is difficult to conceive of the accomplishment of a complex task without the activation of a sufficient number of neurons in the cortex. Neither can one envision the adequate accomplishment of this task without a continuous monitoring of the existing situation with a view toward eventual correction. Keeping in mind the complementarity of these diverse elements, we will now concentrate our attention on the functioning of the brain in the task of planning and executing an action.

Role of Specific Areas of the Cortex

In a series of original experiments, neuropsychologists have demonstrated the complementary functions associated with the elaboration of a plan for task accomplishment, execution, and the supervision of execution. For example, in patients with frontal lobes intact but with damaged parietal lobes, an inability to execute operations required by a plan of action stored in the frontal lobes can be observed (Luria, 1973, pp. 219–220). When these patients are asked to state the steps in their solution to a problem of the type "If there are 10 books on a shelf, and 5 are taken away and 3 added, how many will be left?," these patients generally experience little difficulty in stating the steps involved, if told the necessary steps to take beforehand. However, they experience major difficulties in executing the particular operations required as sub-steps of the problem.

On the other hand, it is most difficult for patients for whom the frontal lobes have been severed but for whom the parietal lobes are intact to suggest the steps of a plan necessary for resolving the arithmetic problem above and even more to supervise the execution of that plan. However, these patients experience little difficulty in executing the sequence of operations when they are taken step-by-step through its execution.

Similarly, in the area of speech, it has been observed among patients whose frontal lobes are intact but for whom the temporal lobe has been severed, that they have the ability to lay out the plan for a speech, but are unable to verbalize the ideas in the plan. An analogous situation results with a patient whose frontal lobes are intact, but where the motor area has been incapacitated.

Thus, we can deduce that the parietal lobes are essential for the executive function, while the frontal lobes seem essential for the planning of the steps in the first place. The temporal lobe's functioning seems to be a prerequisite for producing adequate structures for speech. Similarly, the brain's motor areas are required for actually making the sounds of speech. While in the normal person each of these brain functions is occurring, cases of malfunction demonstrate the need for a coordination of brain functions to succeed with accomplishing a complex task.

Hierarchical Aspects of Task Accomplishment

Having analyzed the behavior of certain types of patients for whom certain areas of the brain have been severed and having deduced the functions handled by specific brain areas, neuropsychologists have hypothesized the complementary roles of these different functions for the accomplishment of a particular task. Cognitive scientists have considered the accomplishment of a task, even the most routine, as being hierarchical (see Albus, 1979; Minsky, 1986; Rosenbaum, Kenny, & Derr, 1983; Simon, 1981a & b; Weiss, 1969). According to these researchers, in accomplishing a given task, information is passed from one area of the brain to another in a fashion similar to a message transmitted from the general to the common soldier during military maneuvers (Albus, 1979). During the accomplishment of a motor task, for example, a global plan of the task to be executed is created in the frontal lobes. From there signals are then transmitted to the pre-motor area, where appropriate patterns of actions are activated. These patterns contain the programming necessary to execute the global movements: movement of an arm or straightening the head, for example. The brain then emits signals to activate the motor neurons responsible for certain movements. This hierarchical functioning of the human information processing system has been illustrated and described in detail by Weiss (1969) in the case of motor tasks, but this pattern seems to apply just as well in operational and verbal tasks (Luria, 1973). This hierarchical structure promotes economical mental functioning, since the same operational, verbal, or motor sub-procedures are combined and re-utilized for the accomplishment of various tasks.

Partial Model for the Accomplishment of a Task

With this explanation in mind, we can now propose a partial model for the processing of information by the cortex during the accomplishment of complex tasks. The chaining of information in this model is illustrated by the diagram in Figure 10.

In this diagram, the boxes represent functions assumed by different areas of the brain, and the arrows suggest possible sequences for activating these functions during the accomplishment of particular tasks. Thus, box 1 represents the plan-generating function, principally carried out through procedures contained in the frontal lobes. In the case of a motor task, like starting a gas-powered lawn mower, these procedures allow the undertaking of sub-procedures necessary for the accomplishment of the global task (Rosenbaum, 1991). In the case of accomplishing a task, like giving a speech, the task includes the identification and the arrangement of the major parts of the speech. In the case of a strictly operational task, such as solving an arithmetic problem, the person outlines or elaborates the possible stages in the problem solution. It is this capability to program action or to develop complex plans, so highly developed within human beings, that makes them intellectually superior to other forms of animal life. The reader should note here that our

Figure 10. Partial model of task planning and execution.

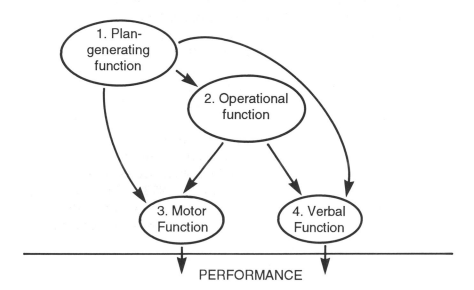

analysis is of a very general nature, and that human thought is much more complex.

Box 2 illustrates the operational function in action. The operations executed involve arithmetic or logic and are apparently carried out in the parietal lobes. In this case, the function of the parietal lobes is analogous to that of the arithmetic and logic units of the central processing unit of a computer, where the task consists of executing the logical or arithmetic operations of a program. Once completed, the task is then returned to other mental units where additional work is performed.

Before we further examine the operational, motor, and verbal function, we should emphasize once again that the diagram in Figure 10 can conceal by its simplicity the complexity of the actual accomplishment of a real task. For example, the principle of hierarchical action applies not only to the generation of plans and their execution through the verbal and motor functions, but this principle also is embodied within tasks specific to each of these functions. The execution of complex operational procedures, as was noted earlier, presupposes the existence of sub-procedures. This observation applies also for the accomplishment of motor or verbal tasks.

Box 4 (verbal function) represents the function necessary for the selection and the execution of phonetic and syntactic *patterns* necessary for an individual to speak in sentences. This function is mostly assumed by the left temporal lobe. Box 3 illustrates the function necessary in the execution of motor patterns, handled by the premotor and motor areas of the cortex.

In the diagram of Figure 10, certain possible consequences of execution are suggested by the arrows connecting the boxes. These sequences demonstrate the accomplishment of different types of tasks. Thus, by the sequence 1-2-3, we suggest that the accomplishment of a global task requires the formulation of a plan, the execution of abstract operations, and the use of motor programs. It is probably in this order that one would expect the person recently taught to drive a car with a manual clutch to shift gears for the first time. For each gear change, the person must think through a new plan of action to undertake, carry out this mentally or at least simulate necessary operations, and finally make the appropriate movements.[3] After several years of driving, one would suspect that the role of the operational function would be limited and that only functions 1 and 3 would enter into play.[4]

Similarly, a person starting to learn a foreign language must think through the plan of discourse that he or she will take during a conversation. The person must then put into action the logical flow of the argument and construct patterns (phonetic, articulation, syntactic) in the necessary sequence 1-2-4 (see Koestler, 1968, Chapter 2, for a good layman's explanation of Chomsky's theory concerning the planning of speech). After several years, one could argue that information processing necessary for sentence construction will become easier and thereby will become an unconscious process.

---

[3] We believe that most human actions are simulated before being executed. When the simulation is judged satisfactory, the action is carried out and results in performance.

[4] We make allusion here to the interesting phenomenon of competencies evolving over time. If accomplishing a task consists of changing an existing situation to a desired one, we could postulate that a person who has accomplished a given task in several phases no longer needs to represent for himself the intermediate situations in all their details. In this situation, the accomplishment of the task limits itself almost completely to the execution of appropriate operations.

Perceptual Function

At the beginning of the chapter, we suggested that the affective, perceptual, and action programming functions could not be considered separately. In order for the neural network to be activated, the affective component must be in place. In order for a task to be accomplished, from the beginning and throughout execution, the organism must stay informed of the current situation in view of an eventual change.

To the diagram in Figure 10 we need to add a perceptual component, as shown in Figure 11. Among other functions, this component will serve in the representation of the desired situation, the initial situation, and the steps along the way.

Figure 11. Global model for task accomplishment.

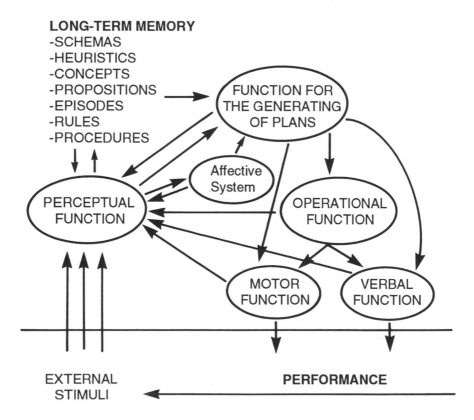

In interpreting Figure 11, it is important to emphasize the tie that exists between the individual's perceptual function and his or her operational, verbal, and motor function. This function's role consists not only in the representation of external situations, but also in the internal representation of hypothetical intermediate situations during the programming of an action.

Global Model of the Accomplishment of a Task

The analysis undertaken during this chapter and the preceding one now allows us to propose a global view of the accomplishment of a task by a human being. These phases include the representation of the existing situation, that of the desired situation, and that of the generation of a plan and then executing and making adjustments to this plan.

In referring to the diagram in Figure 11, we can postulate that during the first phase of the accomplishment of a complex task, the perceptual function is activated, and the individual represents the actual and the desired situations by means of schemas possessed in long-term memory. These representations are made in the form of concepts, propositions, episodes, and other blocks of knowledge. In order that such representations are even possible, it is necessary that the individual possesses the pertinent schemas and an adequately developed information processing system to assign the appropriate concepts to these schemas.

During planning, the system controlling plan generation searches for production rules applicable to the initial situation in order to transform it into an intermediate situation. This process iterates again and again until a sequence of intermediate situations ties the beginning condition to the desired one (the goal). Throughout the assembling of the plan, diverse stages of development are simulated. Operations of the components are mentally executed, and the result of this execution is registered in the perceptual system with a view to eventual rectification. The fact that in practice this process often proceeds in anything but linear fashion, with ample numbers of stops and starts, should be kept in mind.

During this phase of an individual's planning, at least two possibilities can present themselves, depending upon whether the individual has available an appropriate plan or not. In the case of having a plan, the role of the plan generator is simplified: it limits itself to amending an existing plan. In the other case, the plan generator must select appropriate production rules and then create a means permitting the bridging of the gap between initial and desired situations. During the work of putting into sequence the production rules, different heuristics are used by the plan generator. For the work of generating plans to even be possible, the person accomplishing the task must possess both the representations of the actual and of the desired conditions and the appropriate order in which to use the production rules. In the case of the accomplishment of original tasks, it is necessary that the individual possess the appropriate heuristics in order to represent to himself the actual situation or the desired situation, and take the necessary steps to generate a plan.

During the third phase of task accomplishment, the activation of operational, motor, and verbal systems generally results in a performance that can be corrected up to the desired level of expertise. It goes without saying that the execution of the procedures necessary for this phase requires that the information processing system have available and make use of appropriate operations.

The model that we propose to describe the accomplishment of a complex task on the part of a human being takes its inspiration from that of Newell and Simon (1972), Card, Moran, and Newell (1983), and Taylor and Evans (1985). For these researchers, knowledge acquired by the individual is stored in long-term memory in declarative and (or) procedural categories. Based upon these knowledge structures, the function of plan generation is carried out. As a result of this process, performance occurs.

Summary

Whenever we as individuals perceive a gap between reality and our expectations, we develop a plan, the realization of which can be expected to bridge that gap. To do this, we use a personal system of information processing. This system consists of a set of hierarchical functions where procedures are activated during the planning and execution of a task.

More precisely, during the accomplishment of a task, we first represent the existing and the desired condition. Step by step, a plan is conceived by the action programming function. Throughout the development of the plan, this plan is simulated mentally. If necessary, it is adjusted. Once executed, this process results in performance.

During the planning of action, we call upon knowledge stored in long-term memory. The accomplishment of a complex task is thus made possible by the use of declarative and procedural knowledge from our individual repertoires. The work of putting to use these knowledge structures during plan elaboration is guided by the strategies for problem solving that we possess.

Questions: Chapter 4

For review:

(1) In some recipe books you find a picture of the meal you want to prepare, a list of the ingredients that are necessary, and a description of the steps to follow. In this case, how would you identify the current situation, the desired situation, and the plan of the task to be accomplished?

(2) In what portion of the brain are the affective, perceptual, and executive functions concentrated?

(3) Explain the hierarchical processing of the functions in completing a complex task. In what portion of the brain are each of these general functions performed?

(4) How do you relate the concepts of "task accomplishment" and "competency"?

For reflection:

(1) How would you explain the "mental preparation" that athletes like divers or gymnasts do just before executing their maneuvers? How will this activity differ for the novice and the champion?

(2) Do our New Year's resolutions make a difference in our performance in the coming year if: (a) they are seldom referred to; (b) they are frequently referred to; or (c) our spouse wrote them for us?

Chapter 5

Human Competence

There is the clay atop the wheel. It turns ... See the form rising. Do you understand? It forms itself before your eyes. Your eyes, your thumb, your hand, the clay, the wheel, speed: all must be mixed in the right doses to make the right vase. And at the same time, you are thinking.

Jean Giono, *Fullness of the Days*, 1943

Theoretical Foundations

The Concept of Competency

If we agree with the notion that accomplishing a task means transforming an existing situation into a desired one, we can say that whoever is able to carry out these procedures to make such a transformation possesses a competency. We will define a competency as *the capability of an individual to accomplish a given task;* or, more specifically, as *a set of procedures and sub-procedures activated during the planning and execution of a given task.*[1] A person who possesses the requisite competencies for a given situation we term *competent,* and the quality or state of being competent we term *competency.*

In fact, we can distinguish "virtual competency" from "working competency." In the first case, a competency presents itself in the form of declarative and procedural knowledge stored in long-term memory. In the second case, the knowledge has been activated and permits the representation of existing, intermediate, and desired situations, and also the generation and simulation of plans. Working competence in action can be demonstrated mentally (e.g., thinking through to a problem solution) or in a behavioral act (e.g., writing out the steps leading to a problem solution). Thus, we can think of a competency as a set of procedures, the execution of which presupposes the existence of declarative knowledge. We can classify competencies into two major categories: "reproductive-type" competency, and "productive-type" competency," each divided into its own subcategories. We will define *productive-type competency* as that necessary for the accomplishment of

---

[1] We consider that there is a certain analogy between a competency and a computer program. The computer program generally contains a master procedure which when activated, sets off the execution of appropriate sub-procedures. Our definition of competence is in some ways analogous to that of Landa (1983).

tasks for which the plan of execution is not known beforehand. *Reproductive-type competency* will be defined as skill and knowledge necessary for task accomplishment for which the plan of execution is known beforehand. Reciting a poem memorized beforehand is a reproductive-type competency; composing a poem is a productive-type competency.

Productive- and Reproductive-type Competencies [2]

If we consider the accomplishment of a given task as requiring first the researching of an order of execution of a set of procedures and sub-procedures, we have to acknowledge the existence of different planning modalities. As was suggested in the previous chapter, the problem solver must know the sequence of sub-procedures to execute or must herself be able to search them out. In the first case, we say that the problem solver possesses a reproduction-type competency because she uses a known sequence of sub-procedures to accomplish the task (Greeno, 1973). In the other case, the problem solver possesses a production-type competency because she has to discover the order in which sub-procedures must be executed to accomplish the task. Searching out an order of execution presupposes, then, as we have seen in Chapter 3, the mastery of a special type of procedure, heuristics, that we can consider as production rules of a higher order.

Reproductive competencies can be subdivided into two categories: simple and complex. We say that when simple reproductive competencies are activated, a well-defined plan already exists in the individual's long term memory. In the case of complex reproductive competencies, we say that a global plan for task accomplishment exists, and that this plan requires certain adjustments during task accomplishment (Frederiksen, 1984). A good example of a complex reproductive competency is the solution of linear equations. Individuals who accomplish such a task know that, in the larger sense, they have to transform the initial equations given into a set of equivalent equations until they have isolated the unknown. The problem solver thus has an idea of a plan to use, but does not know, before resolving the equation, the exact series of operations to execute.

---

[2] See also Brien & Duchastel (1986).

It is just for convenience that we classify competence into categories. In reality, it more closely resembles a continuum than a dichotomy. At one extreme, we find the competencies that allow for automatic accomplishment of a task, and at the other extreme, we have the competencies required for completely original tasks (see Richard, 1990; Hoc, 1988).

Varied Competencies

Whether it is reproductive- or productive-type competencies under consideration, we suggest that they can be composed of operational, verbal, or motor procedures. Without developing an entire taxonomy of human competencies, we can, by synthesizing the previous arguments, suggest the diverse modes of existence of a competency. This reflection will lead us to formulate specific suggestions for instructional objectives and to see the structuring of content of an instructional activity in a new light.

When representing graphically the reproductive-type competencies, acquired by an individual for routine operational, verbal, or motor tasks, in Figure 12 below, we will use (r) to represent the set of necessary procedures to retrieve, activate, and control the execution of a plan that is within the repertoire of the person accomplishing the task. Next, we will use (o) to stand for the set of procedures necessary to execute the abstract operations of the task (if there are any), and by (–o) to represent the absence of necessary procedures; by (m) the set of procedures necessary to accomplish, if there are any, the motor part of the task and by (–m) the absence of such procedures; by (v) the set of procedures necessary, if there are any, for the verbalization of the task, and by (–v) the absence of such procedures. We now have a tree of possibilities of the different combinations of procedures that characterize the many human competencies.

An examination of Figure 12 suggests several different types of reproductive competencies. For example, the competency to add whole numbers of different lengths can be considered as a reproductive competency implying the execution of abstract operations without

Figure 12. Alternative procedures for executing reproductive-type competencies.

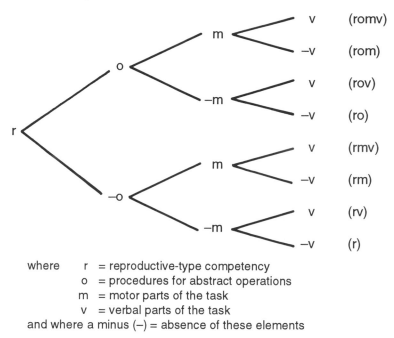

where   r = reproductive-type competency
           o = procedures for abstract operations
           m = motor parts of the task
           v = verbal parts of the task
and where a minus (–) = absence of these elements

necessarily verbalizing anything, (ro),[3] while the competency to recite the story of "The Little Red Hen" can be defined as being of the reproductive type requiring the execution of verbal operations (rv). Along the same lines, the competency to "build a piece of furniture according to a known plan" can be considered as being of the reproductive type requiring the execution of abstract operations (the calculations needed to make the piece of furniture) and motor operations (rom).

The analysis of production-type competency is more complex. In this case, the competencies can be illustrated as in Figure 13.

The diagram in Figure 13 can be easily understood because we have simply modified the first element of the previous diagram. The initial variable (r) representing the procedures to retrieve, activate, and control a known plan has become (p) representing the heuristic procedures

---

[3]   One way of describing a particular competence begins by indicating if it is of the reproductive or a productive type. Next, depending upon the case, the necessity for executing abstract, motor, or verbal operations is determined.

Figure 13. Alternative procedures for executing productive-type competencies.

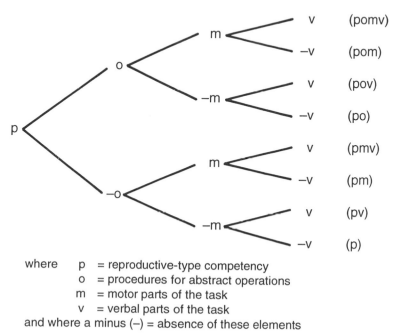

where	p	= reproductive-type competency
	o	= procedures for abstract operations
	m	= motor parts of the task
	v	= verbal parts of the task

and where a minus (−) = absence of these elements

necessary in the design of such a plan. The competency of a person capable of improvising an explanation of a given subject can be traced out as a *production-type competency requiring the execution of abstract operations* (logical operations needed to put together the argument) *and verbal* (pov). The competency to solve story problems involving algebraic equations can also be classified in this category, since in this case the person must work out the plan for the solution, execute a series of abstract operations, and communicate the result. The competency of someone who can create an original work such as a painting or a sculpture can be considered as of the *production-type requiring the execution of abstract and motor operations* (pom).

In addition, one must emphasize the fact that it is by convention that we class competencies into categories. In reality, these exist along a continuum rather than as a dichotomy. At one end of the continuum are the competencies that allow for automatic task accomplishment; and, on the other side, the competencies that permit the accomplishment of original tasks. An alternative classification scheme offering similar results is provided by Jones, Li, and Merrill (1990b).

Competence to Communicate a Given Content

Most of the examples proposed in earlier chapters are related to the acquisition of competencies, as characterized by the execution of abstract or motor operations in a given domain. What about the competencies used for communication?

The person who can define a concept, explain an event, or describe a procedure attempts to inform another person of this concept, event, or procedure. The message sender must then help the receiver move from an existing to a desired cognitive structure. To communicate effectively, the sender must take into account the initial cognitive structure of the receiver and, using the proper rules of communication, deliver the message in a manner that will lead the receiver to construct the desired cognitive structure. Within this frame of reference, competence to communicate must be seen as being of the same order as that of an operational or motor competency; in each case, it is necessary to transform an initial state to a desired state by means of appropriate operations. In the case of a motor competency, the actor operates on a given physical environment by means of physical operations while, in the case of a verbal competency, he acts on a given cognitive structure by means of verbal operations (Searle, 1969; Suchman, 1987).

Along these same lines, communicative competence can be of the reproductive or productive type. In the first case, the sender knows beforehand the order in which messages must be sent (having already heard the messages or having already given them internally a certain order); in the other case, the person must make use of appropriate heuristics to make up the plan of a presentation.

Applications to Instruction

In developing instruction, the formulation of instructional objectives is fundamental. On one hand, well-defined objectives help in the structuring of the content of the instructional activities. On the other hand, objectives allow the trainer to orient instructional activities in such a way as to facilitate the acquisition of specific content. But these objectives do not just help the designer or the trainer. When they are formulated in comprehensive terms, objectives help the *learner* to focus his or her own information processing on the acquisition of well-defined competencies, throughout the learning process, and to track personal progress toward the acquisition of these competencies. In the sections that follow, we make certain prescriptions for the writing of instructional objectives. Following that, working within the framework provided in previous chapters, we will examine the structuring of content for the instructional activities.

Formulation of Instructional Objectives

For Mager (1984) an instructional objective must contain (1) an action word that describes the performance expected of the student, (2) a description of the conditions in which this performance will be measured, and (3) a criterion for measuring completion. We believe that this notion must be broadened to include both mental processing as well as overt behavior. These three components remain in the formulation of an objective, but the present ones must be formulated more in terms of the *activation of mental functioning* of the person accomplishing a given task. The method of defining instructional objectives proposed here is similar to that suggested by Briggs (1977). The difference resides in the fact that we have placed ourselves clearly within a cognitive perspective. Thus, an instructional objective must contain a description of the situation existing at the moment of activation of a competency. The objective must mention if the task to be accomplished is of the reproductive or productive type and if it requires the activation of abstract, motor, or verbal operations. Finally, the objective must describe the desired situation or the product of task accomplishment. It seems to us that the writing of objectives, as we conceive it, overcomes some of the gaps objected to by certain critics (e.g., Eisner, 1985).

To formulate instructional objectives from such a perspective, work must be done in two stages. We begin with the description, generally imprecise, of the performance to expect and then attempt to respond to the questions below. Next, we ensure that the components suggested by Mager are present in the objective.

1. What is the initial or present situation?

2. Does the person who will be undertaking the task have a plan for accomplishing it, or must a new plan be formulated each time the task is accomplished?

3. Is the task to be accomplished characterized by the execution of intellectual operations in a particular domain of knowledge?

4. Is the task to be accomplished characterized by the execution of motor procedures in a given domain?

5. Does the task to be accomplished require verbalization of a given domain?

6. What is the desired situation, or what will be the result of task accomplishment?

While not holding this sequence to be absolute, this type of analysis provides a reasonably clear idea of the content of competencies to be acquired and allows for the formulation of instructional objectives. In the paragraphs below, we provide two examples of objectives using the suggested procedure. The first objective belongs to the culinary arts (making appetizers), and the second to that of geometry (proving theorems). These objectives have been written in two parts: in the first part (before the first parenthesis) comes an action verb describing performance; in the second (in parentheses) we respond to the previously given questions and describe the conditions and criterion level of performance. While these objectives have been formulated in this manner, they can be used in different contexts without major modifications. Thus, when these objectives are given to administrators or to students, only the first part of the objective need be presented. When the objectives are used by designers and content specialists, they will have all the important components:

The student will be capable of preparing different kinds of appetizers (hors-d'oeuvres). (The food and the necessary extra items will be presented to the student, who must prepare ten different types of hors-

d'oeuvres. He or she will not have access to books of recipes, but will prepare the appetizers following the techniques and models presented in the course. The person needs to succeed with eight of the ten types prepared to the satisfaction of judges specially trained for the occasion.)

This task requires a reproductive-type competency, because it is expected that the student will follow recipes taught in class. Both the execution of abstract operations (measurement of quantities, time in cooking, etc.) and the carrying out of motor functions are implied in this performance. In another context the competency required could be different. In formulating the objective, emphasis could be upon the initiative and creativity of the student. In this case, we would expect that the student would "create" new types of appetizers more than reproducing the patterns of others. The objective for geometry is as follows:

The student will demonstrate theorems from Books 1 and 2 of Euclid. (Twelve propositions not demonstrated in class will be presented to the student, who must demonstrate them as written theorems. Of the twelve attempted, ten must be shown successfully).

Here a productive-type competency is required, because the student must employ in acceptable fashion the theorems learned in Books 1 and 2 of Euclid. He or she must execute abstract operations (arithmetic and logic operations) and must execute verbal operations, since acceptable geometric terminology is required in presenting the demonstrations. Thus, we have a productive-type competency with the emphasis upon executing abstract and verbal operations. But if the propositions had been previously demonstrated in class, this competency would have been of the reproductive type. At the other extreme, one could conceive a case where none of the elements of Euclid's geometry would have been taught beforehand in class. In this case, the instruction would have been oriented toward the acquisition of the type of competency that Euclid himself must have possessed.

The Structuring of Content

We suggested in Chapter 3 the means possible to facilitate the encoding of declarative knowledge such as concepts, propositions, and episodes, as well as procedural knowledge, to include simple production rules, procedures, and heuristics. In a typical course, there are large bodies of declarative and procedural knowledge that students or trainees would like to acquire. Thus, during the preparation of instructional activities, the problem consists of identifying declarative and procedural knowledge to be acquired and carefully selecting an order of presentation that will facilitate acquisition. Here are several guidelines to help in knowledge acquisition.

Table of Instructional Contents

We consider a competency to be a set of procedures and sub-procedures used in the accomplishment of a task. As we put together the content of a course, we need to ask ourselves exactly what prior knowledge the student must possess to master a given competency. On one hand, the person who accomplishes the task made possible by the competency must have the declarative knowledge necessary to represent for himself the actual situation, the desired situation, and positions in between. These knowledge structures are concepts, propositions, episodes, and other cognitive units that we attempt to build during learning or which already make up the individual's repertoire. On the other hand, the person who accomplishes a task must make use of procedural knowledge to transform an existing situation into one that is desired. Such knowledge consists of production rules, procedures, and heuristics. Once these knowledge units have been identified, just as schemas facilitating encoding, we can ask ourselves which identifying sequences are likely to facilitate acquisition.

A simple way of identifying the knowledge necessary to accomplish a given task and to determine an optimal order of knowledge acquisition consists first of (a) describing the steps taken by an expert while accomplishing such a task; and (b) identifying and describing the present and desired situations, as well as the intermediate steps necessary for the learner to make the transformation from the one to the other. Next, (c) we identify the declarative and procedural knowledge to be used in representing these entities. Finally, (d) we build a table of instructional contents of the knowledge to be taught.[4] An example of this progression will help clarify the explanation.

Let us imagine, for example, that we wish to teach accounting students how to "complete the federal income tax forms." To begin with, we would describe the task as it would be accomplished by an expert.[5] In our particular case, the task can be described as follows:

(1) Calculate the gross income (by adding the income from various employers, pensions, free-lance work, etc.).

(2) Calculate the deductions (by adding the different donations, costs of child care, union dues, etc.).

(3) Calculate the exemptions (by adding the personal exemption, to that for spouse and dependents if applicable).

(4) Calculate the taxable income (by subtracting deductions and exemptions from gross income).

(5) Then calculate the tax according to the tax tables.

(6) Calculate the tax to pay ... or the refund to expect (by subtracting the total withheld from the total amount of taxes, according to the tables).

Once the task has been described, we can identify the initial situation and the desired situation, as well as the transformations needed to move from the one to the other.

In the case of the tax calculation, the beginning situation consists of a form to fill out and numerical data about a client (net salary, various deductions and exemptions) appearing on various forms and receipts

---

[4] The table of instructional contents makes reference to virtual competencies (declarative and procedural knowledge stored in long-term memory). When the learner has interacted with an instructionally appropriate environment, he will possess working competencies to make possible the desired performance.

[5] Several techniques can be used to describe this sort of task. For more information about these techniques, see Zemke & Kramlinger (1987).

(e.g., W–2 forms). The situation desired is a completed tax form giving the amount of tax to pay or the reimbursement to be received.

The principal transformations to be accomplished are the computation of: (1) the gross income, (2) the taxable income, (3) the deductions, (4) the exemptions, (5) the income tax according to the tables, and (6) whether there is additional tax to be paid or a refund to be received.

Having completed the descriptions of the task, the initial situation, the desired situation, and the principal steps to take along the way, we need to identify the declarative and procedural knowledge that the learners will need to acquire (key concepts and propositions, episodes, simple production rules, procedures, pertinent heuristics and schemas). Next, we draw up a table of declarative and procedural knowledge to be acquired, taking care to keep in mind the suggestions made in Chapter 3 regarding the representation of different declarative and procedural knowledge forms. For our case, the table of instructional contents for the presentation of knowledge could be as follows:[6]

    (1) The concept of tax
    (2) Basic schemas (see explanation below)
    (3) Concepts of gross income
         –income from different employers
         –pensions (e.g., income from Social Security)
         –income from free-lance work
    (4) Procedure for calculating gross income
    (5) Concepts of deductions
         –child care expenses
         –union dues
         –mortgage interest
         –charitable contributions
    (6) Procedures to calculate deductions
    (7) Concepts of exemptions
         –basic personal exemption
         –married persons filing jointly
         –dependents
    (8) Procedure to calculate the exemptions
    (9) Procedure to determine taxable income

---

[6] In certain cases, it is preferable before drafting the table of instructional contents to construct a network of knowledge to be learned (Brien, 1983).

(10) Procedure to calculate taxes, according to the tables
(11) Procedure to calculate tax to pay
(12) Procedure for filling out the form

After having given a definition of the concept of tax, we present several schemas related to the calculation of tax (the calculation of tax is a *process* that is executed in a number of steps; the tax to pay is *calculated based upon net income*; the tax to be paid is *proportional* to net income, etc.).[7] Next, we can present the concepts of gross revenue, deductions, and exemptions, in each case explaining the sub-categories of the concepts. In each case, once the concept has been defined, we can proceed with teaching the procedures related to calculating the item.

After the learner has mastered the different concepts and the procedures associated with each, we can then teach him to calculate the taxable income, to compute tax with the tables, and to follow procedures to determine the tax due. We finish the instructional sequence by explaining to him the way to fill out the tax form.

For instructional purposes, we have deliberately chosen a simple task to analyze. (Those of us who persist in filling out our own tax forms may wonder at times just how simple this process really is!) In practice, it is most common to analyze tasks which themselves contain sub-tasks. In this case, we will be interested to work through an initial breakout of the task into sub-tasks before using the previously described procedures. For example, we can break out any particular job into its principal functions and then break each of these functions into tasks, as is shown in Figure 14. Finally, following the proposed techniques, we analyze the bottom of the task hierarchy and we then build the table of contents for declarative and procedural knowledge required to acquire the needed competencies.

The previous explanation regarding the structuring of content of instructional activities takes us naturally to an emphasis on the importance of prerequisite knowledge in instruction.

---

[7] We are assuming that the learner possesses the prerequisite knowledge regarding "proportional relationship" and the concept of "net income."

Figure 14. Break-out of a job into functions and tasks.

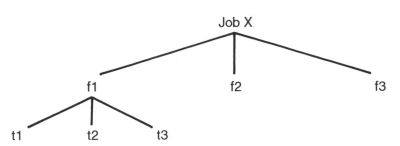

Summary

To bridge the gap between reality and a desired state, the human being undertakes the accomplishment of diverse tasks. When the person can accomplish these tasks, we say that he or she possesses the appropriate competencies. We can define a competency as a set of procedures and sub-procedures used during the accomplishment of a given task.

It is useful to differentiate among knowledge, competency, and performance. The following set of distinctions is helpful: knowledge is data stored in long-term memory, permitting the individual to represent for himself or herself certain objects and events and to act upon these objects and events. A working competency is the capacity of an individual to make use of his or her repertoire of knowledge to develop plans that, once activated, result in a performance. Performance is the result of activation of a competency.

Human competence is differentiated by the different procedures and sub-procedures used during the planning and execution of a task. These competencies are of the reproductive type when they require the use of a known plan. They are of the productive type when a new plan must be devised for each new accomplishment of a task. Reproductive- and productive-type competencies include operational, verbal, or motor components.

During the formulation of instructional objectives, it is important to indicate whether the performance required in the objective is of the reproductive or of the productive type. It is also important to note whether the desired competency requires the execution of abstract, motor, or verbal operations.

When we want to teach someone a given competency, we must describe the task as it would be accomplished by someone possessing the competency. Then, we should identify the beginning situation, the desired situation, and the transformations needed to move from the one to the other. And, finally, we should identify the needed declarative and procedural knowledge and draw up an instructional table of contents.

Questions: Chapter 5

For review:

(1)   Distinguish between knowledge, competence, and performance.

(2)   Distinguish between reproductive- and productive-type competencies. Which is similar to programming a computer and which to executing a program?

(3)   John has been teaching non-parametrics statistics for two months to a group of future statisticians. He has been showing, with audio-visual media, how to use different statistical tests, but he has never had his students solve problems. At the end of the instruction session, he evaluates his students' ability to solve written problems using the various statistical tests explained in class. Given this situation, (a) what kind of competencies is John evaluating with the test he is giving his students? and (b) what kind of competencies will the students be able to demonstrate at the end of their instruction?

(4)   You will find below a brief description of different kinds of performance. Indicate, for each performance, the competency that makes it possible. For example: "add two digit numbers" would be labeled RO (reproductive operations necessary). When classifying the performance, think in terms of emphasis placed on one component or another. You should be aware that in some cases the performance is not detailed enough to make the classification easily.
  (a)   Calculate the area of a triangle following procedures learned in Course XYZ. _____
  (b)   Type a 5-page text. _____
  (c)   Apply the technique of rescue breathing (mouth to mouth resuscitation). _____
  (d)   Write the biography of Marie Curie. _____
  (e)   Describe the carbon cycle in nature. _____
  (f)   Analyze a literary text. _____
  (g)   Plan out an environmental protection campaign. _____

For reflection:

(1) State important questions a designer should reflect upon while formulating learning objectives.

(2) List jobs that require competencies of the reproductive type and jobs that require competencies of the productive type. For each category, list jobs in which there is emphasis upon the execution of abstract operations, motor operations, and verbal operations, or a mix of these.

(3) Considering how easily computers can execute algorithms or known procedures, what are your predictions for the composition of the labor force in developed countries in the 21st century?

(4) Why do most human beings have a tendency to accomplish tasks for which they already know the plan (e.g., putting together an elaborate puzzle, knitting a sweater)?

(5) Recognizing that job classifications may require both productive- and reproductive-type competencies from the same individual, consider the social consequences of assuming responsibility entailed in the use of productive competencies in the following settings:

  (a) Military: enlisted soldier vs. officer or NCO (Non-Commissioned Officer).
  (b) Academic: teaching assistant vs. faculty member.
  (c) Medical: paramedic vs. doctor.

Could it be that members of both groups exercise productive competencies but work within a broader or narrower range of options?

Chapter 6

Acquisition of Competence

For a thousand years, we have played with wings and beak to gather fish heads, but from now on we will have a reason to live: to learn, to discover, and to be free.

Richard Bach, *Jonathan Livingston Seagull*, 1970

Introduction

When an individual does not possess the competency necessary to complete a given task, a natural step is to become involved in learning activities. These activities will then modify the existing cognitive structure to provide a more viable one. When the person has acquired the necessary knowledge and can put it to use in the accomplishment of a task, we say that he or she has acquired a competency. It is at this point in the acquisition of a competency that we concern ourselves most particularly in this chapter. We will study first the different phases of acquiring a competency as suggested by Fitts and Posner (1967), and we will propose a simple model for the acquisition of competencies based on the understanding built up in the previous chapters. And, finally, we will formulate recommendations to help in setting up appropriate learning activities.

Theoretical Foundations

Phases in the Acquisition of a Competency

In his book *The Architecture of Cognition*, Anderson (1983) builds on the work of Fitts and Posner (1967) regarding the acquisition of a competency. For Anderson, the phases proposed by Fitts and Posner for learning of motor competencies can be compared to learning a competency involving the execution of abstract operations.

In the first phase (cognitive phase), knowledge structures are stored in a declarative form by the individual. If it concerns the acquisition of the competency necessary to drive an automobile with a manual transmission, for example, using schemas presently available, the individual encodes propositions regarding the positions of the different gears and the body movements required to shift gears.

During the second phase (associative phase), the acquired knowledge is deepened. The individual learns to use certain facts related to shifting gears. No longer does the declarative aspect of knowledge prevail, according to Anderson, but rather the procedural. This emphasis, however, does not prevent the person from retaining in memory the declarative knowledge that helped to form the procedural base. In other words, the person can now shift gears or describe how to do so, based upon knowledge stored in memory.

In the third phase (automatic phase), the competency is refined or sharpened progressively. The procedures are carried out with much more flexibility, and the individual no longer needs to think carefully about how to do it. This last phase can continue over several years, and it is at this level of competence that we can distinguish the novice from the expert, because the expert's performance is so much more adept. It is thus interesting to note that during this phase, the individual generally loses the ability to verbalize the facts stored during the first phase.

A Modified Version of Anderson's Model

Keeping in mind the model proposed by Anderson and the discussion leading up to it in the preceding chapters, we can consider the acquisition of competence as occurring in three complementary phases. These phases are: motivation, assembly, and refinement. We present here the process of acquisition of a competency as being carried out in three consecutive phases, but in reality these processes occur more often in parallel, overlapping to some extent. Thus, if we maintain that motivation must be present during the acquisition of a competency, we must conclude that the effect of motivation must persist throughout the acquisition of competence in order to accomplish the tasks related to encoding and refinement. Similarly, operations involved in the assembly of knowledge for mastery of a competency also occur during the refinement phase.

Motivation

In the first place, the individual perceives a gap between reality and a desired state or, alternatively, a gap between the existing cognitive structure and the desired cognitive structure. If one cannot accomplish a task that would satisfy one's needs, the motivation to acquire the necessary set of competencies to accomplish that task goes beyond a certain threshold and will be activated.[1] Therefore, one mentally constructs an expected set or a representation of the desired condition and is now ready to put forth the effort necessary to change an existing cognitive structure to a more appropriate one. The person now becomes an active learner and can become engaged in the assembly phase of a competency.

Assembly

In the previous chapter, we defined a competency as a set of procedures and sub-procedures activated during the planning and accomplishment of a task. During the assembly phase of a given competency, the learner must acquire the knowledge needed to represent the actual condition, the intermediate conditions, and the desired condition. The person must also acquire the knowledge necessary to change the actual into the desired condition. This line of reasoning leads us to view the assembly of a competency as a process going on with two complementary phases, as is suggested by Anderson: (a) encoding of the declarative aspect of the procedures and sub-procedures of a competency, and (b) encoding of the procedural aspect of these procedures and sub-procedures.

Encoding the declarative aspect. During the encoding of knowledge in a declarative form, the schemas useful for assimilating the information from the outside are activated. The perceptual function assigns values to the variables of these schemas. The schemas necessary for the learning of concepts, propositions, production rules, algorithms, and entire bodies of knowledge are thus brought up and filled with content. These schemas generate knowledge in the categories of concepts, propositions, episodes, production rules, or heuristics that are stored in long-term memory for eventual use in developing plans. According to Anderson (1983), at this stage, the individual will make certain trials at encoding the procedural

---

[1] We define expectations as mental representations possessed by the individual of what she can accomplish after learning, as well as benefits that will accrue as a result of this accomplishment, e.g., more security, higher esteem in the eyes of others, self actualization, etc. Thus, expectations are representations of desired situations.

part of the competency. Heuristics of the most general sort are put to profitable use at this stage of work.

Encoding of the procedural aspect. Next, knowledge acquired in declarative form, including production rules, is put to use by the plan-generating function. In the accomplishment of a task, such as the solving of linear equations in algebra, production rules are applied to the initial equation in such a way as to transform it (by means of operations contained in the rules) into a series of equivalent equations until the equation is solved. In learning to drive an automobile with a manual gear shift, the motor operations contained in the production rules are carried out. In the writing of a text, the necessary operations for constructing sentences must be executed.

Thus, in the case of the acquisition of a rule of production, a schema pertinent to encoding the rule will be activated and the appropriate values assigned to the schema variables. The rule will be simulated, corrected if necessary, and finally, the operational, motor, or verbal functions of competence activated. When the required competency consists of defining a concept, the schema for encoding a concept will first be called up and values will be assigned to the variables of this schema. Next, a plan will be activated to formulate the definition. This plan may consist of: (1) indicating the classification of the concept, and (2) enumerating the characteristics of the concept. Next, the verbal and motor components will be activated to formulate the necessary definition.

Modalities of knowledge encoding. According to Rumelhart and Norman (1978), the encoding of knowledge is done using different modalities. These researchers have termed the activity learning by "accretion" when a schema exists in the individual's repertoire that can directly assimilate the information presented. In this case, a direct correspondence is established between the schema and the externally presented information. The components of the perceived message are assigned to the schema variables, and the result is a new element of knowledge. It is this type of learning that occurs during everyday communication.

On the other hand, a number of situations exist for which the individual possesses no appropriate schema. In this case, the person undertakes learning by restructuring. Several schemas in the person's repertoire are first combined or integrated to constitute a new schema more representative of reality. This process of restructuring, dealt with by Ausubel (1968), cannot be thought of without considering the complementary processes of assimilation and accommodation described by Piaget (1967) and Salomon (1982).

Refinement

After several times of using a particular competency, executing the procedures component is done automatically. It is during this phase that a competency acquires a degree of finesse that characterizes expertise (Erickson & Smith, 1991). We can suppose that during this phase of repeating the procedures, the function of simulation will be partially or totally short-circuited.

Applications to Instruction

Supporting the Acquisition of a Competency

Keeping in mind the model proposed previously and drawing upon theoretical work by Gagné (1984), we can suggest a number of recommendations for a trainer facilitating the three phases of acquisition of a competency: motivation, assembly, and refinement.

Support for motivation. In order for an individual to put forth the effort required to acquire a given competency, he or she must understand that the promised competency will permit the direct or indirect satisfaction of felt needs. The designer and the person conducting instruction first must propose a content that responds to the individual needs of participants. The teaching should include events that will trigger the formation of expectations.[2] Presenting the objectives of a course and

---

[2] We distinguish the *methods* and the *media* of teaching. We define a method of teaching as a way of carrying out the "events of instruction" (in the sense meant by Gagné, 1984). These events include the presenting of information, questioning, and providing feedback. Media are supports used to carry out these same events. While a particular medium is frequently associated with certain specific methods, for some methods it is possible to use another medium than that generally assigned. For example, in using the case study

describing the advantages that will follow the acquisition of the competency envisioned are among the actions taken by a trainer to develop expectations. It is worth noting that once expectations are triggered, they should be fulfilled, or on the next instructional cycle, credibility will suffer.

Support for assembly. Because a competency is built of a series of procedures and sub-procedures activated during the accomplishment of a task, the support to give during the assembly of a competency is to lead the learner to represent the initial, intermediate, and desired conditions, and to combine the sub-procedures already possessed to structure the new competency. We present first the definitions, as pronouncements to activate the schemas necessary in the accomplishment of a task, as well as the appropriate production rules. In addition, during the assembly phase, we encourage the learner to encode the procedural aspect of a competency by means of exercises, followed by appropriate feedback. For example, in a course in auto mechanics, after learning the parts of the carburetor, the trainee is asked to take apart and reassemble the apparatus, thus becoming familiar with appropriate procedures.

Support for refinement. Assembly of a competency generally results in nothing more than an outline or skeleton of a competency. To be of any real utility, a competency must be refined. While recognizing that this process may extend over a period of years, nonetheless, the designer or the trainer will give the learner opportunities to practice a competency by frequent exercises or other methods of activating competencies. It is by such exercises that the learner puts into action procedures for locating, retrieving, and transferring information. The trainer should furnish appropriate feedback to permit the improvement of the competency, in the kind of role we identify with a coach in athletics.

These various directives regarding the support to give during the refinement of a competency lead us to emphasize the distinction between the assembly and the refinement of a competency. In the case of assembly, it is a question of shaping the competency, while in refinement, it is a matter of perfecting a competency and refining it. In

---

method, the presentation of the case could be given verbally by the trainer or by using videotape. Similarly, tutorial instruction may be maintained by use of a human tutor or by interaction with a computer, at least in certain cases.

any given domain, the difference between the performance of a novice and that of an expert is that the expert has competence that has been shaped, exercised, and refined until the desired level of expertise has been attained, while the novice does not.

Let us return to our example of learning to shift gears in a driver's training course. To begin with, the learner is at the level of needing to learn to shift gears on a car with manual transmission. To help in the shaping of a competency, the instructor could demonstrate the proper procedures, urge the student to carry out the needed movements, and give specific feedback.

Next, to sharpen this competency, the instructor would set up varied occasions to practice this competency: on level or hilly terrain, under various traffic conditions, etc. Normally, the phase of refinement is the final phase in the acquisition of a competency. If this is not the case, it will be necessary to resume the process while varying the explanations and the exercises.

Choice of Appropriate Teaching Methods

Several methods of teaching can be used to facilitate the acquisition of a given competency. Certain of these methods facilitate the acquisition of reproduction-type competencies, while others favor production-type. We propose, in Tables 1 and 2, the classification of a certain number of these methods, and in Appendix A, give brief descriptions of them (see also Brien & Dorval, 1986, and McKeachie, 1986). This classification takes into account the type of competency to be acquired (reproductive- or productive-type competency, requiring the execution of abstract, verbal, or motor operations), the modality of desired instruction (individualized instruction, or small or large groups), and the declarative or procedural aspect of the competency to be acquired.

Using this classification is relatively simple, since the designer or the trainer has already identified the desired competencies and the declarative or procedural knowledge elements necessary for the acquisition of the competencies identified in instructional tables of contents.

Table 1. Acquisition of reproductive-type competencies.

Competence	TYPE OF INSTRUCTION		
	Individualized	Small groups	Large groups

With an operational component	Guided readings (d)
	Adjunct auto-
	  instruction (d, p)
	Information
	  mapping™
	Audio-visual
	  modules (d, p)
	Programmed
	  instruction (d, p)
	Televised
	  instruction (d, p)
	Tutorial (d, p)
	Project method (p)
	Exercises (p)
	Simulations (p)
	Protocols (p)
		Games (d, p)
		Case method (p)
		Project method (p)
		Peer tutoring (d, p)
		Simulation (p)
		Demonstration (d)
		Role playing (d, p)
			Lecture (d)
			Demonstration (d)
			Contests (p)
			Games (d, p)
			Peer tutoring (d, p)

With a verbal component	Guided readings (d)
	Adjunct auto-
	  instruction (d, p)
	Information
	  mapping (d, p)
	Audio-visual
	  modules (d, p)
	Programmed
	  instruction (d, p)
	Televised
	  instruction (d, p)
	Tutorial (d, p)
	Project method (p)
	Exercise (p)
		Games (d, p)
		Case method (p)
		Contests (p)
		Discussion (d, p)
		Peer tutoring (d, p)
		Demonstration (d)
			Games (d, p)
			Peer tutoring (d, p)

With a motor skills component	Audiovisual
	  modules (d, p)
	Televised
	  instruction (d, p)
	Tutorial (d, p)
	Demonstration (d)
	Exercises (p)
	Protocols (p)
	Simulations (p)
		Demonstration (d)
		Peer tutoring (d, p)
		Simulation (d, p)
		Contests (p)
			Demonstration (d)
			Contests (p)
			Peer tutoring (d, p)

Table 2. Acquisition of production-type competencies.

Competence	TYPE OF INSTRUCTION		
	Individualized	Small groups	Large groups
With an operational component	Guided readings (d) Adjunct auto- 　instruction (d) Information 　mapping (d) Audio-visual 　modules (d, p) Programmed 　instruction (d, p) Televised 　instruction (d, p) Tutorial (d, p) Project method (p) Exercises (p) Simulations (p) Protocols (p)	Games (p) Case method (p) Project method (p) Discussion (p) Simulation (p) Demonstration (d) Role playing (d, p)	Lecture (d) Demonstration (d) Contests (p) Games (d, p) Peer tutoring (d, p)
With a verbal component	Guided readings (d) Adjunct auto- 　instruction (d, p) Information 　mapping (d, p) Audio-visual 　modules (d, p) Programmed 　instruction (d, p) Televised 　instruction (d, p) Tutorial (d, p) Project method (p) Exercise (p)	Games (d, p) Case method (p) Contests (p) Discussion (d, p) Peer tutoring (d, p) Demonstration (d)	Lecture (d) Demonstration (d) Contests (p) Games (d, p) Peer tutoring (d, p)
With a motor skills component	Audiovisual 　modules (d) Televised 　instruction (d, p) Tutorial (d, p) Demonstration (d) Exercises (p) Protocols (p) Simulations (p)	Demonstration (d) Peer tutoring (d, p) Simulation (d, p)	Demonstration (d) Contests (p) Peer tutoring (d, p)

When teaching the material for the first time, it is important to determine the constraints within which the instruction must be prepared and delivered. Is there considerable time for course preparation? Is it easy to get the learners together? How limited are the finances? These are the kinds of questions the designer or the trainer should be asking in order to identify the constraints.

Once the constraints have been determined, the designer must choose, using the kinds of options suggested in Tables 1 and 2, one or more appropriate methods to teach the required competencies. Once chosen, the following considerations must be taken into account.

First, we must keep in mind the fact that certain methods can simultaneously facilitate the encoding of both the declarative and the procedural components of a competency—i.e., items displaying (d, p) in Tables 1 and 2. Other methods seem more often to favor the declarative component (d) or else the encoding of the procedural component (p). Thus, we can use programmed instruction as a unique method for improving learners' competency to add whole numbers (reproduction-type competency with an operational component), since this method can improve encoding of the declarative and procedural parts of this competency. In addition, using one method to improve the declarative part of a competency and another for the procedural part is possible. Thus, to teach how to "solder a copper pipe" (reproduction-type competence with motor components), we could first provide a demonstration to handle the encoding of the declarative component, then provide exercises to build the procedural component of this competency.

Second, during the use of these tables, we must work to support encoding of the declarative part of a competency following a given modality of instruction (individualized instruction, or small or large groups) and the encoding of the procedural part following another modality. This case is frequently encountered when, in class, the teacher provides a demonstration (good for obtaining a declarative reproductive-type competency) related to the way "to make subject and predicate agree" and then provides exercises (good for procedural productive-type competencies) to complete as homework.

Regarding the utilization of Table 2, we should remind the reader that production-type competencies are characterized by the mastery of heuristics. Consequently, to facilitate the acquisition of these heuristics, the learner must be encouraged to combine or to adjust abstract, verbal or motor operations. This requirement presupposes that the learner has already mastered, up to a certain point, the appropriate sub-procedures, or alternatively, that he or she already possesses the reproduction-type competency necessary. For example, if we wish to lead the learner to acquire the heuristics needed to demonstrate geometric propositions, we must first be certain that he or she has mastered the concepts (including definitions), and the necessary production rules. Before employing any of the methods suggested in Table 2, in most instances, we will employ the methods promoting acquisition of reproductive-type competencies.

Finally, we must emphasize the fact that the proposed classification is given only as a recommendation. The choice of instructional methods, like that of structuring the content of an instructional activity, returns us to the problem of using or not using a "recipe" or formula for instruction. In both cases, we must search out a set of operations that will help move an individual from cognitive structure X to structure Y, which requires the mastery of instructional heuristics for which, we must admit, our knowledge is limited.

Summary

In order for the learning of a competency to take place, the person doing the learning must be motivated. The person must understand that the learning undertaken will allow satisfaction of real needs, in the short, medium, or long term.

We can show that the assembly of a competency takes place in two phases. First, the declarative portion of a competency is encoded. Once this has been achieved, the individual can generally communicate verbally the acquired knowledge elements, but still cannot adequately accomplish the required task.

Subsequently, an encoding of the procedural aspect of the competency is required. The functions related to the planning and execution of action are then exercised. The learner uses planning to process the knowledge in his or her repertoire to change the existing to a desired situation.

The most salient modes of encoding knowledge are accretion and restructuring. Encoding completed by accretion occurs when the individual possesses schemas in his repertoire capable of assimilating presented information, with little modification of those schemas required. When the individual does not possess the appropriate schemas, he or she builds new schemas through a modification or combination of existing schemas.

After assembling the competency, the stage of refinement of the competency remains. The new competency is adjusted until it allows an adequate accomplishment of the required task.

Several instructional methods can be used to promote the assembly and refinement of a given competency. In order to make a wise choice of methods, factors such as the type of competency to be acquired, the declarative or procedural aspect of the competency, and the appropriate mode of instruction must be taken into account.

Questions: Chapter 6

For review:

(1) What are the phases in the acquisition of a competency? Illustrate by using the acquisition of a particular competency, such as pole vaulting, speaking a foreign language, or replacing the brake shoes on a car.

(2) What are the two subphases in the assembly of a competency?

(3) What is learning by accretion? How does it differ from learning by restructuring? What activities might an instructor incorporate into his or her teaching to support each of the three stages of the acquisition of a competency?

(4) During the past two weeks, John has been offering a training session for new salespersons on how to sell cars. He mainly used lectures, video, and demonstrations as instructional methods. What phases of the acquisition of a competency are not supported by this training? What instructional methods should be used to complete his training?

For reflection:

(1) A common fault of university teachers is treating their subject matter as entirely declarative knowledge and not taking time to refine the competencies taught. Aside from inciting a revolution, how could this pattern be changed?

(2) A competency enables someone to accomplish a given task. Accomplishing a given task implies transforming an initial condition into a goal state or desired condition. Given this set of circumstances, try to explain the difference between novice and expert in a domain of your choice.

(3) Try to identify in your surroundings instructional situations that
     have defects in terms of the attention paid to motivation, assembly
     (declarative and procedural aspects), and refinement.

Chapter 7

Applications to Instruction

But without technique, a talent is nothing but a distracting habit.[1]

Brassens, *La Mauvaise Réputation*, 1954 (translation)

---

[1] This statement of Brassens can be applied to the domain of training if we change "a talent" to "a theory."

Introduction

In preceding chapters, we have offered suggestions regarding the design and practice of particular components of an instructional activity. Suggestions have been given for the formulation of instructional objectives, the structuring of course content, and the choice of appropriate methods of instruction. These suggestions, shown as a set of questions in Appendix B, can be useful to the teacher in preparing for class, but also they can and should be integrated into the overall process of course design.[2]

Systematic Design of an Instructional Activity

The ways in which information is transmitted today have seen considerable change from the days when humans lived entirely from cultivating the soil or from hunting and fishing. Given that only a few centuries have passed since all knowledge was conveyed orally, and for the most part on an individual basis, it is rather amazing to see today's multitude of communication modes, ranging from a simple programmed text to options for mass communication reaching millions of individuals simultaneously.

Not only have the modes of transmission of knowledge been radically transformed, but also the means of designing and preparing instructional activities have evolved considerably. A complete technology has been developed, permitting the systematic study of instructional needs, the

---

[2] For a detailed study of the process of designing an entire training system within the framework of Gagné & Briggs, the reader is invited to consult Gagné (1984), Gagné & Briggs (1979), and Merrill, Li, & Jones (1990).

formulation of instructional objectives, the structuring of content, the choice of methods and media of instruction, as well as the evaluation of instruction itself. These techniques have been restructured and are used in what is called *instructional design* (e.g., Banathy, 1991; Briggs, Gustafson, & Tillman, 1991). This preparation generally takes place by following the stages depicted in Figure 15.

Figure 15. Systematic design of instruction.

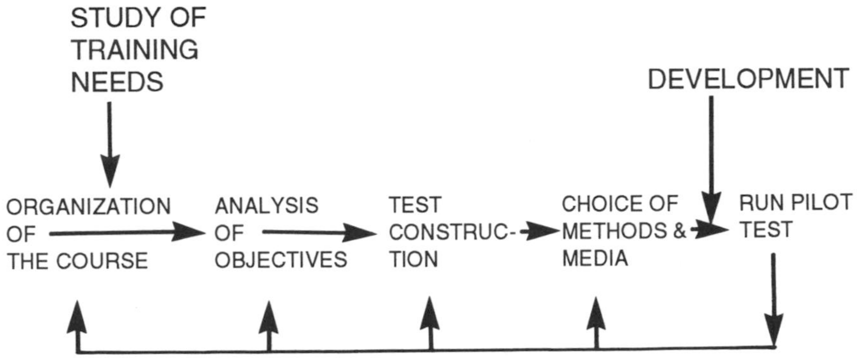

Study of Instructional Needs

Through consultation with interested stakeholders, the designer of instructional activities attempts to make explicit the competencies that the course or the program of studies to be developed propels us toward learning. This step of studying needs constitutes the starting point for an instructional activity.

Example

Because of certain pressures exerted by parents, governmental authorities, and teachers themselves, a decision is made to revise the program of teacher certification. A study of needs is then conducted to poll opinions of teachers, parents, and the leaders of scholarly commissions. A consensus is eventually obtained relative to the competencies and attitudes expected for both preservice and inservice teachers. These competencies are described in the form of general announcements, an example of which might be: "At the end of the instructional program, the preservice teacher will be familiar with various teaching applications of the computer."

Course Organization

The designer responsible for elaborating a course in a given domain proceeds then to more explicitly identify the competencies and attitudes that learners must acquire in the course. In collaboration with one or more content specialists, the designer specifies the goals of the course, the objectives or themes, and the terminal objectives of the various units of the course (in other words, the different parts of the course). These objectives are formulated in the form of performance that the learners must demonstrate. The designer then proceeds with the organization of the course.

Example

The organization, in terms of goals and objectives, of a course about the instructional uses of the computer could be presented as follows:

Course title: The Microcomputer and Instruction.

Course goals: At the completion of instruction, the student should be able to:

–explain, along the major lines, the working of the computer and its diverse instructional applications;

–demonstrate a positive attitude toward the use of the computer for instructional ends.[3]

Unit 1:   Overall functioning and brief history of the computer.

Unit 2:   Instructional applications of the computer.

At the core of the first unit, the terminal objectives could be:

1.1. Describe the overall functioning of a computer and its principal components. (The student will not be allowed to consult course notes. In a description in two or three pages, he or she will need to adhere closely to content presented in the course).

1.2. Write a brief essay of the history of the computer and its applications in instruction. (The student will not be allowed to consult course notes, but will be required to trace, in two or three pages, the historical evolution of the computer following the major lines suggested in class. He or she will be expected to use the definitions given in class.)

---

[3]   The basic computer course will be designed to enable the learner to experience positive emotions throughout the entire course. Assuming that these emotions are positive, they are subsequently translated into positive attitudes toward instructional applications of the computer (see Chapter 2). Of course, the particular attitudes and prior experience of the learner will be crucial (e.g., a learner with a past history of bad experiences with computers might have a different experience, and have certain emotional blockages to be overcome, than a person starting out afresh). Assuming that these emotions are positive, they are subsequently translated into positive attitudes toward instructional applications of the computer (see Chapter 2).

Analysis of Terminal Objectives

Once the course has been organized, the designer proceeds to analyze the terminal objectives of the different course components or units. This task attempts to identify the content elements necessary for the attainment of terminal objectives, and searches for an appropriate sequence of instruction. The instructional table of contents in Table 3

Table 3. Instructional table of contents.

```
THE MICROCOMPUTER
Introduction
        Concept of microcomputer
                Overall structure of the course
Physical components (hardware)
        Internal components
                Microprocessors
                        Control unit
                        Arithmetic and logic unit
                Central storage
                Random access memory (RAM)
                Read-only memory (ROM)
                Interfaces
        External components
                Input units
                Output units
                Input-output units
        Software
                Basic software
                        Machine language
                        Assembly language
                        Higher level languages
                Application software
                        Common applications
                        Educational software
        Test construction
```

draws upon the macro-structure of the first part of the first unit of the course, the different knowledge elements to be acquired, and the order in which the acquisition of the cognitive units could be facilitated.

It is at this stage that the designer builds the assessment tools as well (tests of prerequisites, pre-test, post-test) that will be used to determine the effectiveness of the course when put into practice. The questions which make up these different tests will obviously have to be compatible or congruent with the different course objectives.

Example

Some examples of questions that are compatible or congruent with terminal objectives 1.1 and 1.2 could be:

a. Describe the overall functioning of a computer and its principal components, as presented during the course.

b. Write a brief history of the computer's use in instruction, as presented during the course.

Choice of Instructional Methods

The designer now has on hand all the necessary elements to make a choice of the appropriate instructional methods. This choice should be based upon the terminal objective(s) of the course.

In making the choice, the designer should identify the methods which will facilitate motivation and then allow for assembly and refinement of the competencies in the instructional table of contents. He or she should then write out the scenario of the course or of the lesson, targeting the acquisition of these competencies. In turn, this scenario allows the elaboration of a prototype to be pilot tested with a sample population.

Example

In regard to module 1—which enables the attainment of objective 1.1 (Describe the overall functioning of a computer and its principal components)—a short explanation will be given in class to learners relative to the content of the module. Learners will familiarize themselves in turn with the structure of the computer by means of explanatory text.[4] After reading this text, learners will move to the laboratory where exercises programmed on the computer regarding this part of the course will be presented.[5]

Pilot Testing

Finally, the designer selects a sample of learners with whom the prototype course can be tried out. Then, corrections or adjustments can be made as needed in the different parts of the course in response to inadequacies noted. This is a particularly important step, as it allows formative feedback and a refinement of the methods of instruction. Following is an example of a detailed Outline of a Teaching Text (see page 124):

---

[4] An outline of the text to be constructed is shown at the end of this chapter.

[5] Particular attention should be given to the choice of exercises in order to avoid frustrating the learner. The activity should be designed in such a way as to bring about pleasant emotions.

Outline of a Teaching Text

The Microcomputer

Introduction

To begin simply we can consider the microcomputer as an electronic apparatus that permits the execution of certain arithmetic and logic tasks by means of a set of instructions defined beforehand. We call this set of instructions a "program." These instructions contain one or more operations to execute (addition, subtraction, comparison, etc.).

Concepts of microcomputer and program.

We will classify the components of a microcomputer into two groups: first, the physical components or the hardware; and second, the programs to be executed or the software. We will first examine the physical components of the microcomputer and then afterward concern ourselves with the software.

Macro-structure of the text

Physical components of the microcomputer

To understand exactly what a microcomputer is and how it functions, we will make use of an analogy:

The system of special requests of the (hypothetical) town of Pleasantville: Suppose that in the town of Pleasantville it is possible to listen, on demand and with a direct broadcast, to your favorite pieces of classical music, and at the same time to observe on your TV screen the orchestra that is playing the pieces. The system of special requests can be illustrated as shown below:

Analogy used to explain the microcomputer's components and functioning

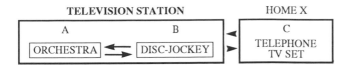

In the diagram, "A" represents an orchestra with its conductor and musicians, "B" represents the room where special requests are received and the announcer by which the special requests of Joe and Jane Doe are transmitted to the orchestra conductor. "C" represents the living room in the home of John and Jane, which is equipped with a TV set and a telephone allowing them to make special requests. Finally, the arrows symbolize the information making its way through the system.

Transmission, execution, and diffusion of a special request: When John or Jane wish to hear Schubert's "Unfinished Symphony," they make a request to the announcer, who then transmits the desired selection to the orchestra conductor. The conductor then leads the musicians in playing the chosen piece, based upon the score in front of him. Both sound and images are played and sent to the home of John and Jane, the waiting listeners.

The principal physical components of a micro-computer: A microcomputer resembles to some extent the system of special requests for Pleasantville. For now, and throughout this explanation, to keep things simple, we will think of a microcomputer as having only three main internal components (the components "under the hood" of the microcomputer) and two external components.

The analogy refers to a system of "special requests" that certain radio channels offer to their listeners

Macro-structure to present the physical components of the microcomputer

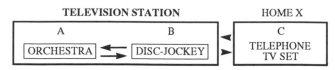

Part A of the diagram represents the central processing unit of the computer or, if you wish, the brain of the microcomputer. It is here that the programs or sets of instructions furnished to the computer are executed. This part is itself made up of two fundamental components: the microprocessor and the central memory.

Concept of central processing unit (CPU)

1. The microprocessor is the component responsible for: (a) interpreting the instructions to be executed (identifying if addition, subtraction, comparison, etc., are required) and (b) executing these operations. We can compare the microprocessor to the link between the conductor and the musicians of the orchestra in Pleasantville, if we agree that the conductor interprets the score and the musicians play it.

Concept of microprocessor

2. The main memory is the place where the instructions are stored that the microprocessor will have to interpret and execute. We can compare the main memory to the musical selection to be played.

Concept of main memory

Part C of the diagram represents the input and output units of the microcomputer. The keyboard from which the instructions are entered in order to make the program run is an input device, and the monitor from which we receive the results of the program is an output unit. We can compare the keyboard to the telephone allowing the transmission of special requests and the television to the monitor where we can observe the results of program execution.

Concept of input-output units

Part B symbolizes the interfaces, consisting of electronic circuits that make possible the communication of information between the input-output units and the brain of the computer. Certain of these interfaces transform the commands typed on the keyboard into electric signals understandable to the brain of the microcomputer, while others transform the orders executed into pictures and text appearing on the monitor (we will return to this subject later). The interfaces play the role of the announcer of the television station which makes possible the communication between the subscribers and the orchestra conductor.

Concept of interfaces

Transmission and execution of a program. When the user wishes to have a task executed by the microcomputer, he or she writes a program (a set of instructions) to be entered from the keyboard (input unit). This program is then carried via the appropriate interface to the main memory.

Description of functioning (process)

Program instructions are thus read and interpreted by the control unit of the microprocessor and transmitted to the arithmetic and logic unit to be executed stored in main memory, and retransmitted to an output unit by means of an appropriate interface.

Questions: Chapter 7

For review:

(1) Give a sequence of activities that would allow a designer to systematically develop a course.

(2) At what point in your reply to the previous question does the designer explicitly: (a) describe the competencies and attitudes that the learner is to acquire; (b) write scenarios for the instruction; (c) make explicit the prerequisite knowledge of the course; (d) field-test the instructional materials?

For reflection:

(1) This chapter made extensive use of an analogy (playing music and the operation of a computer). What are the benefits of such an analogy, and what are its limitations? What were the limits of this analogy's usefulness?

(2) The scientific method is characterized by (a) observation, (b) formulation of hypotheses, (c) experimentation, and (d) correction of the hypothesis, if necessary. Using the model shown in Figure 15, where would you place these activities in the systematic design of instruction?

(3) While designing instruction, the designer works with subject matter specialists. What are the respective roles of these two specialists while engaged in this activity?

(4)   The model for the systematic design of instruction shown as Figure
      15 could be used both by behaviorist and cognitivist designers.
      Aside from the cognitivist's more elaborate mental model of the
      learner, in your opinion, what would be the differences in their
      accomplishment of the various steps?

Chapter 8

Conclusions

Incompetence has no limits, neither in time nor in space.

(Peter and Hull, *The Peter Principle*, 1969)

In his futuristic book *Megatrends*, John Naisbitt noted the major increase in the number of workers in the information sector in the United States.[1] While these occupations constituted 17% of the workforce in 1950, they represented 60% in 1982 (Naisbitt, 1984). This workforce transformation has placed new demands upon instruction and, to meet these demands in the coming years, trainers will need to revise existing ways of operating.

The techniques presently in use must be modified in order to reduce the time required to design an instructional system; and, in these cases, the role of the computer will go well beyond that of the simple word processor so prevalent today. We can envision software to enable the designer to study instructional needs, to formulate course objectives, to analyze and structure the content, and to choose methods and media for appropriate instruction and evaluation. One such project, the I.D. Expert, is currently under development at Utah State University (Merrill, Li, & Jones, 1990) to build the next generation of instructional design tools, in this case as an "expert system" for consultation by the designer. If we assume that these tasks can never be completely automated except to the extent that they are described in a sufficiently precise fashion, and that such a description requires the appropriate theoretical foundation, we must admit that at present the basis for a technology of instruction is too limited.

In effect, this is the foundation of instructional technology that must be rethought and reformulated in the coming years, and this effort, in our opinion, must move beyond the present research completed in cognitive science. We must first agree that the mastery of a given subject matter and the application of instructional techniques alone will not be sufficient to produce quality instruction. As this book has emphasized, designing an instructional system boils down to the task of devising a set of activities

---

[1] The author classifies the following types of occupations within the information sector: programmers, teachers, office workers, secretaries, accountants, salesmen, administrators, insurance workers, government workers, lawyers, and technicians.

permitting the learner to transform an inappropriate cognitive structure into one more appropriate or complete. The accomplishment of this task presupposes also an adequate knowledge of the role of affect in learning, i.e., maintaining that motivation is important. Succeeding at such a task requires problem solving, and presupposes—on the part of the designer—the most accurate representation possible of the ways in which a human being stores, represents, and uses information. The mastery of an appropriate mental model of the learner, including both affective and cognitive components, seems to us to be the cornerstone of quality instruction.

In the preceding chapters, we have attempted to show how the techniques used today to formulate objectives for instructional activities, for structuring the content of a course, and for the choice of appropriate methods can be conceptualized within the context of cognitive science. The recommendations made must stay hypothetical: the concepts proposed will evolve as the field of cognitive science itself matures. In any case, if the hypotheses suggested motivate the learner to become more interested in this new science, as designer, trainer, researcher, or student, our goal will have been attained.

Questions: Chapter 8

For review:

(1) What are some critical concerns, beyond subject matter and instructional techniques, that must be addressed to produce quality instruction?

For reflection:

(1) As we have observed the movement from Computer Assisted Instruction (CAI) to Intelligent Computer Assisted Instruction (ICAI), we see that the concepts upon which the design of these instructional activities are based are changing (from behaviorist to a humanist and cognitivist point of view). Why is this occurring?

(2) In this book we have attempted to provide the reader with an appropriate mental model of the learner. In what directions would you predict that such mental models will evolve in the next decade?

Bibliography

Albus, J. (1979, April). A model of the brain for robot control. *BYTE*, 4:9, 130–148.

Anderson, J. R. (1981). Concepts, propositions, and schemata: What are the cognitive units? *Nebraska symposium on motivation* (Vol. 28). Lincoln: University of Nebraska Press.

Anderson, J. R. (1983). *The Architecture of cognition.* Cambridge, MA: Harvard University Press.

Anderson, J. R. (1984, November). Some reflections on the acquisition of knowledge. *Educational Researcher.*

Anderson, J. R. (1985). *Cognitive psychology and its implications* (2nd ed.). San Francisco: W. H. Freeman.

Anderson, J. (1986). Production systems, learning, and tutoring. In *Production system models of learning and development.* Cambridge, MA: The MIT Press.

Ausubel, D. P. (1968). *Educational psychology: A cognitive view.* New York: Holt, Rinehart, & Winston.

Bach, R. (1970). *Jonathan Livingston Seagull.* New York: Macmillan.

Banathy, B. H. (1991). *Systems design of education: A journey to create the future.* Englewood Cliffs, NJ: Educational Technology Publications.

Barlow, H., Blakemore, C. & Weston-Smith, M. (Eds.) (1990). *Images and understanding.* New York: Cambridge University Press.

Baudet, S. (1990). Relative importance of information and retrieval from memory. In H. Mandl, E. DeCorte, N. Bennett, & H. F. Friedrich (Eds.), *Learning and instruction* (Vol. 22). London: Pergamon Press.

Beer, U. & Erl, W. (1973), *Epanouissement de la créativité*. [Expanding creativity]. Sherbrooke, Canada: Les Editions Paulines.

Bejar, I. I., Chaffin, R. & Embretson, S. (1991). *Cognitive and psychometric analysis of analogical problem solving*. New York: Springer-Verlag.

Bersini, H. (1990). Before and after breakdowns. In *Actes du Quatrième Colloque International "Progrès de la recherche cognitive."* [Acts of the Fourth Internation Colloquium, "Progress in cognitive research"]. Paris: Association pour la Recherche Cognitive [Association for Cognitive Research].

Berlyne, D. E. (1965). *Structure and direction in thinking*. New York: John Wiley & Sons.

Bloom, B. S. (1956). *Taxonomy of educational objectives: Handbook I: Cognitive domain*. New York: Longman.

Bloom, B. S. (1976). *Individual characteristics and school learning*. New York: McGraw-Hill.

Bonnet, C., Hoc, J. M. & Tiberghien, G. (1986). *Psychologie, intelligence artificielle et automatique* [Psychology, artificial intelligence, and automaticity]. Brussels: Pierre Mardaga Editor.

Bower, G. H. (1975). Cognitive psychology: An introduction. In *Handbook of learning and cognitive processes* (Vol. 1). Hillsdale, NJ: Lawrence Erlbaum Associates.

Brassens, G. (1954). *La mauvaise réputation* [The bad reputation]. Paris: Editions Denoël.

Brien, R. (1983, May). Sequencing instruction: A cognitive science perspective. *Programmed Learning and Educational Technology*, 20:4, 102–114.

Brien, R. (1985). Analyse de compétences humaines: Une perspective cognitive. [Analysis of human competencies: A cognitive perspective]. In J. Vazquez-Abad & J. Y. Lescop (Eds.), *La technologie éducative et le développement humain [Educational technology and human development]; Actes du Colloque du CIPTE [Acts of the CIPTE Colloquium]* (pp. 261–269). Québec, Canada: Télé-université, Université du Québec.

Brien, R. (1987, November). Apport des sciences cognitives à la conception d'activités de formation motivantes. [Contributions of cognitive science to the design of motivating instructional activities]. In J. Y. Lescop (Éd.), *Technologie et communication éducatives; Actes du Colloque du CIPTE [Acts of the CIPTE Colloquium]* (pp. 289–300). Québec, Canada: Télé-université, Université du Québec.

Brien, R. (1989). *Design pédagogique: Introduction à l'approche de Gagné et de Briggs* (2e éd.). [Instructional design: Introduction to the approach of Gagné & Briggs]. Québec, P.Q. Canada: Les Editions Saint-Yves.

Brien, R. & Dorval, E. (1986). *Le choix des méthodes d'enseignement: Guide pratique* [The choice of methods of instruction: A practice guide] (Report No. 128). Québec, Canada: Université Laval, département de technologie de l'enseignement [Department of Instructional Technology].

Brien, R. & Duchastel, P. (1986, November). Cognitive task analysis underlying the specification of instructional objectives. *Programmed Learning and Educational Technology*, 23:4, 363–370.

Briggs, L. (1977). *Instructional design: Principles and applications.* Englewood Cliffs, NJ: Educational Technology Publications.

Briggs, L. J., Gustafson, K. L. & Tillman, M. H. (Eds.) (1991). *Instructional design: Principles and applications* (2nd ed.). Englewood Cliffs, NJ: Educational Technology Publications.

Bruner, J. S. (1967). *Toward a theory of instruction.* Cambridge, MA: The Belknap Press of the Harvard University Press.

Bruner, J. S., Goodnow, J. J. & Austin, G. A. (1956). *A study of thinking.* New York: John Wiley & Sons.

Card, S. K., Moran, T. P. & Newell, A. (1983). *The psychology of human-computer interaction.* Hillsdale, NJ: Lawrence Erlbaum Associates.

Chomsky, N. (1956, September). Three models of the description of language. *IRE Transactions on Information Theory*, 113–124.

Cofi, I. M. (1972). *Introduction to logic* (4th ed.). New York: Macmillan.

Demailly, A. & Le Moigne, J. L. (1986). *Sciences de l'intelligence et sciences de l'artificielle.* [Artificial and intelligent sciences]. Lyon: Presses Universitaires de Lyon.

Denis, M. (1987). Imagerie visuelle et répétition mentale. [Visual imagery and mental repetition]. In A. Vom Hofe & R. Simonnet (Eds.), *Recherches en psychologie du sport.* [Research in sports psychology]. Issy-les-Moulineaux: Editions E. A. P.

Denis, M. (1989). *Image et cognition.* [Images and cognition]. Paris: Presses Universitaires de France.

D'Hainault, L. (1980). *Des ins aux objectifs de l'éducation.* [The ends of objectives in education]. Brussels: Editions Labor.

Einstein, A. (1935). *The world as I see it.* New York: Philosophical Library.

Eisner, E. W. (1985). *The art of educational evaluation: A personal view.* Philadelphia, PA: Falmer Press.

Eisner, E. W. (1991). *The enlightened eye: Qualitative inquiry and the enhancement of educational practice.* New York: Macmillan.

Erickson, K. A. & Smith, J. (Eds.) (1991). *Toward a general theory of expertise.* New York: Cambridge University Press.

Farreny, H. (1985). *Les systèmes experts: Principes et exemples.* [Expert systems: Principles and examples]. Toulouse: CEPADUES Editions.

Fitts, P. M. & Posner, M. I. (1967). *Human performance.* Belmont, CA: Brooks/Cole.

Fodor, J. A. (1986). *La modularité de l'esprit.* [The modularity of the mind]. Paris: Les Editions de Minuit.

Fortin, C. & Rousseau, R. (1989). *Psychologie cognitive: Une approche de traitement de l'information.* [Cognitive psychology: An information processing approach]. Québec: Presses de l'Université du Québec.

Fredericksen, N. (1984, Fall). Implications of cognitive theory for instruction in problem solving. *Review of Educational Research,* 54:3.

Gagné, E. D. (1985). *The cognitive psychology of school learning.* Glenview, IL: Scott Foresman.

Gagné, R. M. (1962). The acquisition of knowledge. *Psychological Review,* 69:4, 355–365.

Gagné, R. M. (1977). *The conditions of learning* (3rd ed.). New York: Holt, Rinehart, & Winston.

Gagné, R. M. (1980). Is educational technology in phase? *Educational Technology,* 20:2, 7–14.

Gagné, R. M. (1984). *The conditions of learning* (4th ed.). New York: Holt, Rinehart, & Winston.

Gagné, R. M. & Briggs, L. (1979). *Principles of instructional design* (2nd cd.). New York: Holt, Rinehart, & Winston.

Gallaire, H. (1985, October). La représentation des connaissances. [Knowledge representation]. *Revue La Recherche,* 1240–1248.

Gallway, W. T. (1984). *The inner game of tennis.* New York: Bantam.

Gardner, H. (1985). *The mind's new science: A history of the cognitive revolution.* New York: Basic Books.

Gentner, D. & Gentner, D. R. (1983). Flowing waters or teaming crowds: Mental models of electricity. In D. Gentner & A. L. Stevens (Eds.), *Mental models.* Hillsdale, NJ: Lawrence Erlbaum Associates.

Gentner, D. & Stevens, A. L. (1983). *Mental models.* Hillsdale, NJ: Lawrence Erlbaum Associates.

George, C. (1983). *Apprendre pa l'action.* [Learning by action]. Paris: Presses Universitaires de France.

George, C. (1988). Interaction entre les connaissances déclaratives et les connaissances procédurales. [Interaction between declarative and procedural knowledge]. In Pierre Perruchet (Ed.), *Les automatismes cognitifs.* Bruxelles: Mardaga.

Gineste, M. D. (1986–1987). Les analogies et les métaphores: Leur rôle dans la compréhension de textes informatifs. [Analogies and metaphors: Their role in the comprehension of informative texts]. *Bulletin de Psychologie*, 40, 473–479.

Giono, J. (1943). *Rondeur des jours.* [Fullness of the days]. Paris: Editions Gallimard.

Glynn, S. M., Yeany, R. S. & Britton, B. K. (Eds.) (1991). *The psychology of learning science.* Hillsdale, NJ: Lawrence Erlbaum Associates.

Greeno, J. G. (1973). The structure of memory and the process of solving problems. In R. Solso (Ed.), *Contemporary issues in cognitive psychology.* The Loyola Symposium. Washington, DC: Winston.

Greenwood, J. D. (Ed.) (1991). *The future of folk psychology: Intentionality and cognitive science.* New York: Cambridge University Press.

Hampden-Turner, C. (1981). *Maps of the mind.* London: Mitchell Beazley.

Hannum, W. & Hansen, C. (1989). *Instructional systems development in large organizations.* Englewood Cliffs, NJ: Educational Technology Publications.

Harmon, P. & King, D. (1985). *Expert systems.* New York: John Wiley & Sons.

Helman, D. H. (Ed.) (1988). *Analogical reasoning: Perspectives of artificial intelligence, cognitive science, and philosophy.* Boston: Kluwer Academic Publishers.

Hoc, J. M. (1988). *Cognitive science of planning.* London: Academic Press.

Horn, R. E. (1989). *Mapping hypertext.* Lexington, MA: The Lexington Institute.

Howard, R. W. (1987). *Concepts and schemata: An introduction.* London: Cassell Educational.

Intellectica (1984). Bulletin de liaison de l'Association pour la Recherche Cognitive, Paris, No. 10.

Izard, C., Kogan, J. & Zajonc, R. (1984). *Emotions, cognition, and behavior.* Cambridge, England: Cambridge University Press.

Johnson-Laird, P. N. (1983). *Mental models.* Cambridge, England: Cambridge University Press.

Jones, M. K. (1989). *Human-computer interaction: A design guide.* Englewood Cliffs, NJ: Educational Technology Publications.

Jones, M. K., Li, Z. & Merrill, M. D. (1990, October). Domain knowledge representation for instructional analysis. *Educational Technology*, 30:10, 7–32.

Keane, M. T. (1988). *Analogical problem solving.* New York: Halsted Press.

Keller, J. M. (1983). Motivational design of instruction. In C. M. Reigeluth (Ed.), *Instructional-design: Theories and models.* Hillsdale, NJ: Lawrence Erlbaum Associates.

Keller, J. M. & Burkman, E. L. (1993). Motivation principles. In M. Fleming & W. H. Levie (Eds.), *Instructional message design* (2nd ed.). Englewood Cliffs, NJ: Educational Technology Publications.

Koestler, A. (1968). *Le cheval dans la locomotive.* Paris: Calmann-Lévy.

Koestler, A. (1981). *Bricks to Babel.* New York: Random House.

Krathwohl, D. R., Bloom, B. S. & Masia, B. B. (1964). *Taxonomy of educational objectives: Handbook II: Affective domain.* New York: Longman.

Krishnamurti, J. (1975). *Freedom from the known.* New York: Harper.

Lachance, B., Lapointe, J. & Marton, P. (1979). Le domaine de la technologie éducative. [The domain of educational technology]. *Revue de l'Association pour le Développement de l'Audio-visuel et de la Technologie en Education*, 10–15.

Landa, L. N. (1974). *Algorithmization in learning and instruction.* Englewood Cliffs, NJ: Educational Technology Publications.

Landa, L. N. (1983). The algo-heuristic theory of instruction. In C. M. Reigeluth (Ed.), *Instructional design theories and models.* Hillsdale, NJ: Lawrence Erlbaum Associates.

Langdon, D. G. (Ed.) (1978, 1980). *The instructional design library* (40 volumes). Englewood Cliffs, NJ: Educational Technology Publications.

Lazorthes, G. (1982). *Le cerveau et l'esprit.* [The brain and the mind]. Paris: Flammarion.

Le Ny, J. F. (1979). *La sémantique psychologique.* [Psychological semiotics]. Paris: Presses Universitaires de France.

Le Ny, J. F. (1989). *Science cognitive et compréhension du langage.* [Cognitive science and the comprehension of language]. Paris: Presses Universitaires de France.

Li, Z. & Merrill, M. D. (1990). Transaction shells: A new approach to courseware authoring. *Journal of Research on Computing in Education*, 23:1, 72–86.

Lindsay, P. H. & Norman, D. A. (1977). *Human information processing: An introduction to psychology* (2nd ed.) New York: Academic Press.

Luria, A. R. (1973). *The working brain.* London: The Penguin Press.

Luria, A. R. (1980). *Higher cortical functions in man* (2nd ed.). New York: Basic Books.

Mager, R. F. (1984). *Preparing instructional objectives.* Belmont, CA: D. S. Lake.

Malglaive, G. (1990). *Enseigner à des adultes* [Teaching adults]. Paris: Presses Universitaires de France.

Mandler, G. (1984). *Mind and body.* New York: John Wiley & Sons.

Maslow, A. H. (1970). *Motivation and personality* (2nd ed.). New York: Harper and Row.

Martin, B. L. & Briggs, L. J. (1986). *The affective and cognitive domains: Integration for instruction and research.* Englewood Cliffs, NJ: Educational Technology Publications.

McFarland, T. D. & Parker, O. R. (1990). *Expert systems in education and training.* Englewood Cliffs, NJ: Educational Technology Publications.

McKeachie, W. J. (1986). *Teaching tips: A guidebook for the beginning college teacher.* Lexington, MA: D. C. Heath.

Merrill, M. D. (1983). Component display theory. In C. M. Reigeluth (Ed.), *Instructional design theories and models.* Hillsdale, NJ: Lawrence Erlbaum Associates.

Merrill, M. D. (1987). A lesson based upon component display theory. In C. M. Reigeluth (Ed.). *Instructional design theories in action: Lessons illustrating selected theories.* Hillsdale, NJ: Lawrence Erlbaum Associates.

Merrill, M. D. (1991, May). Constructivism and instructional design. *Educational Technology*, 31:5, 45–53.

Merrill, M. D., Li, Z. & Jones, M. K. (1990a) Limitations of first generation instructional design (ID$_1$). *Educational Technology*, 30:1, 7–11.

Merrill, M. D., Li, Z. & Jones, M. K. (1990b). Second generation instructional design (ID$_2$). *Educational Technology*, 30:2, 7–14.

Miller, G. A. (1956). The magical number seven, plus or minus two: Some limits on our capacity for processing information. *Psychological Review*, 63, 81–97.

Miller, G. A., Galanter, E. & Pribram, K. H. (1960). *Plans and the structure of behavior.* New York: Holt.

Minsky, M. (1986). *The society of mind.* New York: Simon and Schuster.

Naisbitt, J. (1984). *Megatrends.* New York: William Morrow.

Neisser, U. (1976). *Cognition & reality: Principles & implications of cognitive psychology.* New York: W. H. Freeman.

Newell, A. & Simon, H. A. (1956, September). The logic theory machine. *IRE Transactions on Information Theory*, 61–79.

Newell, A. & Simon, H. A. (1972). *Human problem solving.* Englewood Cliffs, NJ: Prentice-Hall.

Nguyen-Xuan, A. & Richard, J. F. (1986). L'apprentissage par l'action: L'intérêt des systèmes de production pour formaliser les niveaux de contrôle et l'interaction avec l'environment. [Learning by doing: The interest of systems of production for formalizing levels of control and interaction with the environment]. In C. Bonnet, J. M. Hoc & G. Tiberghien (Eds.), *Psychologie, intelligence artificielle et automatique.* [Psychology, artificial intelligence, and automaticity]. Bruxelles: Pierre Mardaga, Editeur.

Norman, D. A. (1981). What is a cognitive science? In D. A. Norman (Ed.), *Perspectives on cognitive science.* Hillsdale, NJ: Lawrence Erlbaum Associates.

Norman, D. A. (1982). *Learning and memory.* San Francisco: W. H. Freeman.

Norman, D. A. (1983). Some observation on mental models. In D. Gentner & A. L. Stevens (Eds.), *Mental models.* Hillsdale, NJ: Lawrence Erlbaum Associates.

Norman, D. A. (1988). *The design of everyday things.* New York: Basic Books.

Norman, D. A., Rumelhart, D. E. *et al.* (1975). *Explorations in cognition.* San Francisco: Freeman.

Nuttin, J. (1980). *Théorie de la motivation humaine.* [Theory of human motivation]. Pairs: Presses Universitaires de France.

Ormrod, J. (1989). *Using your head: An owner's manual.* Englewood Cliffs, NJ: Educational Technology Publications.

Ortony, A., Clore, G. L. & Collins, A. (1988). *The cognitive structure of emotions.* New York: Cambridge University Press.

Piaget, J. (1967). *La psychologie de l'intelligence.* [The psychology of intelligence]. Paris: Librairie Armand Colin.

Peter, L. J. & Hull, R. (1969). *The Peter principle.* New York: William Morrow.

Plutchik, R. & Kellerman, H. (1980). *Emotion: Theory, research, and experiences.* New York: Academic Press.

Reigeluth, C. M., Merrill, M. D., Wilson, B. G. & Spiller, R. T. (1980). The elaboration theory of instruction: A model for sequencing and synthesizing instruction. *Instructional Science.*

Richard, J. F. (1984). Résoudre des problèmes au laboratoire, à l'école, au travail. [Problem solving in the laboratory, at school, and at work]. *Psychologie Française*, No spécial.

Richard, J. F. (1985). La représentation du problème. [Problem representation]. In S. Ehrlich (Ed.), Les représentations. *Psychologie Française*, 277–284.

Richard, J. F. (1986a). Traitement de l'énoncé et résolution de problème [Processing of the statement and problem resolution]. In *Bulletin de Psychologie, Jugement et Langage, Hommages en l'honneur de G. Noizet*, 344–351.

Richard, J. F. (1986b). Modèles de traitement de l'information et modèles stochastiques. [Models of information processing and stochastic models]. In A. Demailly et J. Lemoigne (Eds.), *Sciences de l'intelligence sciences de l'artificiel.* Lyon: Presses Universitaires de Lyon.

Richard, J. F. (1990). *Les activités mentales.* [Mental activity]. Paris: Armand Collin.

Rogers, Y., Rutherford, A. & Bibby, P. (Eds.) (1992). *Models in the mind: Theory, perspective, and application.* New York: Academic Press.

Romiszowski, A. J. (1980). Problem solving in instructional design: An heuristic approach. In A. Howe (Ed.), *International yearbook of educational technology 80/81.* London: Kogan Page.

Rosenbaum, D. A. (1991). *Human motor control.* New York: Academic Press.

Rosenbaum, D. A., Kenny, S. B. & Derr, M. A. (1983, February). Hierarchical control of rapid movement sequences. *Journal of Experimental Psychology: Human Perception and Performance.*

Royer, J. M., Cisero, C. A. & Carlo, M. S. (1993, Summer). Techniques and procedures for assessing cognitive skills. *Review of Educational Research*, 63:2, 201–243.

Rumelhart, D. E. (1979). *Analogical processes and procedural representation* (report no. 81). San Diego: University of California, Center for Human Information Processing.

Rumelhart, D. E. (1980). Schemata: The building blocks of cognition. In R. J. Spiro, B. C. Bruce & W. F. Brewer (Eds.), *Theoretical issues in reading comprehension.* Hillsdale, NJ: Lawrence Erlbaum Associates.

Rumelhart, D. E. & McClelland, J. L. (1986). *Parallel distributed processing: Explorations in the microstructures of cognition* (Vol. 1 and 2). Cambridge, MA: MIT Press.

Rumelhart, D. E. & Norman, D. A. (1978). Accretion, tuning and restructuring: Three modes of learning. In *Semantic factors in cognition.* Hillsdale, NJ: Lawrence Erlbaum Associates.

Rumelhart, D. E. & Ortony, A. (1977). The representation of knowledge in memory. In R. C. Anderson, R. J. Spiro & W. E. Montague (Eds.), *Schooling and the acquisition of knowledge.* Hillsdale, NJ: Lawrence Erlbaum Associates.

Salomon, G. (1979). *The interaction of media, cognition, & learning: An exploration of how symbolic forms cultivate mental skills and affect.* San Francisco, CA: Jossey-Bass.

Salomon, G. (1982). *Communication and education: Social and psychological interactions.* Newbury Park, CA: Sage.

Scholer, M. (1983). *La technologie de l'éducation: Concept, bases et applications.* [Educational technology: Basic concepts and applications]. Montréal: Les Presses de l'Université de Montréal.

Searle, J. (1969). *Speech acts: An essay in the philosophy of language.* New York: Cambridge University Press.

Simon, H. A. (1969). *The sciences of the artificial.* Cambridge, MA: MIT Press.

Simon, H. A. (1981a). Cognitive science: The newest science of the artificial. In D. A. Norman (Ed.), *Perspectives on cognitive science.* Hillsdale, NJ: Lawrence Erlbaum Associates.

Simon, H. A. (1981b). *The sciences of the artificial* (2nd ed.). Cambridge, MA: The MIT Press.

Skinner, B. F. (1956). *Science and human behavior.* New York: Macmillan.

Stolovitch, H. & Larocque, G. (1983). *Introduction à la technologie de l'instruction.* [Introduction to the technology of instruction]. Saint-Jean-sur-Richelieu, Québec: Editions Préfontaine.

St-Yves, A. (1982). *Psychologie de l'apprentissage-enseignement.* [Psychology of teaching/learning]. Québec: Presses de l'Université du Québec.

Suchman, L. A. (1987). *Plans and situated actions: The problem of human-machine communication.* New York: Cambridge University Press.

Taylor, J. C. & Evans, G. (1985). The architecture of human information processing: Empirical evidence. *Instructional Science,* 347–359.

Travers, R. M. (1970). *Man's information system: A primer for media specialists and educational technologists.* Scranton, PA: Chandler.

Varela, F. J. (1989). *Connaître les sciences cognitives: Tendances et perspectives.* [Understanding cognitive sciences: Tendencies and perspectives]. Paris: Editions du Seuil.

Vosniadou, S. & Ortony, A. (Eds.) (1989). *Similarity and analogical reasoning.* New York: Cambridge University Press.

Weiss, P. (1969). Central versus peripheral factors in the development of coordination. In K. H. Pribam (Eds.), *Perception and action: Selected readings.* Baltimore, MD: Penguin Books.

West, C. K., Farmer, J. A. & Wolff, P. M. (1991). *Instructional design: Implications from cognitive science.* Englewood Cliffs, NJ: Prentice-Hall.

Wilensky, R. (1983). *Planning and understanding: A computational approach to human reasoning.* Reading, MA: Addison-Wesley.

Zemke, R. & Kramlinger, T. (1987). *Figuring things out* (7th ed.). Reading, MA: Addison-Wesley.

Appendix A

A Sampling of Different Modes of Instruction

Adjunct auto-instruction

Self-instructional material given to the student most often consists of a set of readings to be completed. In the case of adjunct auto-instruction, however, the content is designed to require active participation on the part of the learner. The designer carefully adds questions to already existing texts to ensure that the learner interacts with the material. This system is generally accompanied by a guide suggesting to the learner the readings and the exercises to complete in order to attain the chosen objectives.

Case method

In this method, instruction consists of proposing to a small group (or to one learner) a problem to resolve within a given specialized domain and then guiding the group (or the learner) through the resolution of the problem. The first goal of the case method is to motivate the students to take part in the necessary steps of problem solving and thus to promote the assimilation of these steps.

Demonstration

This is a method of teaching used to illustrate a principle, process, or action. A demonstration most often consists of a presentation by the instructor of models, apparatus, films, etc. During the presentation, the instructor can underline important points in the demonstration. In addition, it is often an opportune time to illustrate "the wrong way" to do something.

Educational games

This is a method of instruction in which the learning activities are created within the framework of pre-existing or specially designed games. Competition among the players makes the activities of learning more stimulating, breathing life into activities that might otherwise be rather dull.

Guided readings

This method provides an individualized method of instruction in which information is presented by means of specially chosen texts. When seen as a system, the interaction involved in this method is rather limited, with the student primarily receiving information from the system. Typically, the student must complete a certain number of readings in order to attain the objectives previously established. This system is generally accompanied by a guide suggesting to the learner the appropriate readings and the exercises to complete.

Lecture

This is a method of teaching in which the content is presented through spoken discourse to a group of students (usually a large group). This method provides an effective overview of material before students proceed with individual study. While a lecture can facilitate the encoding of concepts from a given subject matter, it is generally not effective in the refinement or the connection of mental constructs acquired. When the refinement of skills is necessary, a lecture session can best be followed by exercises, games, or by the use of other methods which promote performance.

Modularized mediated instruction

This method of individualized instruction occurs when information is conveyed by means of different media (text, audiotape, video, slides, microcomputer). Generally a guide providing directions to the activities is given to the student, as well as an exercise workbook to help in the mastery of the content presented.

Programmed instruction

While in adjunct auto-instruction a lesson is given based upon already existing material, with programmed instruction a new set of structured content must be created. Two classic forms of programmed instruction are described below, linear versus branching types:

Linear programmed instruction: This method of individualized instruction provides the content by means of a finely graduated text. The text is divided into chapters containing sequences of items or of elements, each consisting of sentences to complete followed by appropriate feedback (one or two words). In linear programmed instruction, the zones of information are reduced to a minimum. The student is asked to complete sentences. One or more words (the correct response) are then provided by means of a correction key. Linear programmed instruction is based on B. F. Skinner's theory of operant conditioning. In recent years this method has fallen into some disuse due to the difficulty of structuring content in sufficiently large amounts to maintain interest (i.e., avoid being mechanical and boring) and at the same time not overreaching the memory limits of the student for specific words or phrases.

Branching programmed instruction: This is a method of individualized instruction in which the content is provided through a specially designed text. Generally, the text is divided into chapters and sections. Each section contains a particular "zone of information," followed by a multiple-choice question. Among the responses suggested, one is correct and the others are plausible but incorrect. With each choice is a direction of a particular page to turn to. If an incorrect response is chosen, the student will be directed to the appropriate section to clear up the misunderstanding, while the choice of a correct response will direct the student toward the next zone of information in the text.

Project method

In the case method, a problem is posed to an individual or a small group with the intent of obtaining a solution. In the project method, the solution envisioned to solve the problem must also be applied to the completion of a project or work of some sort.

Role playing

This method of instruction requires the simulation of a situation in which interpersonal relations play an important part. Within the framework of this situation, learners assume different roles with the goal of eventual resolution of conflict. Such exercises can be handled through face to face communication, or via computer or computer-assisted videodisc (multimedia) presentation.

Simulation

This method of instruction puts at the learner's disposition a model of a physical, social, administrative, or other phenomenon, and gives the learner the possibility to act on this model and then observe the consequences of decisions made. In some cases, we can combine the characteristics of simulations with those of games (see educational games) to infuse more interest on the part of the learner. This result we would call simulation-games.

Structured information

The presentation of content requires definitions, explanations, examples, exercises, and so forth. Generally, these components are not easily identified in the instructional material provided to the student. This lack of clarity is not the case in structured information, where the instructor has carefully identified each component of content to make of it a "specific block." In this way, a person studying a given text can more easily locate the elements desired. This means of presentation has certain advantages during review and later consulting of a particular text by the learner (see Horn, 1989).

Tutoring

This method of teaching provides course content by means of tutors chosen from among the students of one group as a result of their mastery of the content and their ability to communicate this content to others.

Video instruction

This is a method of individualized instruction in which information is conveyed by means of video cassettes. The instruction also includes a guide providing additional information, as well as an exercise notebook (or worksheets) allowing the learner to verify the attainment of lesson objectives.

Appendix B

Important Questions

Competencies to be Acquired

Are the competencies to be acquired in this instructional activity of the productive or reproductive type?

Do these competencies require the execution of abstract, verbal or motor operations, or combinations of these types?

If there are specific attitudes to be acquired during this instructional activity, have they been identified?

Structuring the content

Will the learner participating in this instructional activity have mastered the prerequisite competencies (will he or she possess the key schemas, concepts, propositions, etc.) to assist in acquiring the desired competencies?

Has the order of presentation of the competencies to be acquired been carefully considered?

    a.   Is there a macro-schema that can be used to help anchor the set of competencies to be acquired?

    b.   Are there particular schemas that can be used to facilitate the encoding of competencies to be acquired?

c.   Will the competencies taught in this activity draw upon concepts or propositions not seen previously in the activity?

Teaching competencies

Have activities been included to enhance the learner's motivation?

a.   Does the learner understand what use the learning of these competencies will be?

b.   Is the size of the learning task given to the students too large or too small?

c.   Have the emotional effects the learner will feel during the learning activities been considered?

Have the appropriate activities for promoting the assembling of the competency been thoroughly considered?

a.   Have the activities favoring the encoding of the declarative component of this competency been planned?

b.   Have the activities promoting the encoding of the procedural component of the given competency been thought through?

Have the activities enabling the refinement of competency been included?

Glossary

action verb: verb used in the formulation of a learning objective in order to describe the targeted performance.

adaptive organism: living organism possessing a mechanism enabling it to adjust to the environment.

analysis of objectives: one step of the instructional design and development process, consisting of the identification of the declarative and/or procedural knowledge to be learned, the establishment of links between cognitive units, and the determination of learning sequences that may facilitate learning.

artificial intelligence: one of the cognitive sciences; its goal is the understanding of intelligence behavior by its simulation (generally on a computer).

attitude: internal disposition of a person toward objects, persons, or situations that influences the choice of his or her actions.

body of knowledge: an organized set of declarative and procedural knowledge related to a particular subject or set of subjects.

cerebral cortex: part of the human-brain whose functions include the formulation and monitoring of action plans.

chain of expectancies: a sequential set of states or expectations that leads toward a desired expectancy or goal state.

cognitive evaluation: positive or negative evaluation made when a gap has been perceived between a given and a desired situation or state.

cognitive psychology: one of the cognitive sciences; its goal is the understanding of behavior by the observation of subjects' performances.

cognitive science: science oriented toward the goal of understanding intelligent behavior. Cognitive science is at the intersection of cognitive psychology, artificial intelligence, linguistics, neurosciences, and philosophy.

cognitive structure: set of interrelated cognitive units that a person possesses at a given time. These cognitive units are stored in long-term memory.

cognitive unit: declarative and/or procedural knowledge (e.g., concepts, propositions, episodes, production rules, procedures, heuristics, schemata).

competency (complex reproduction-type): competency which requires the modification or adaptation of an already known global plan in the accomplishment of a given task.

competency (production-type): competency which implies the elaboration of a new plan in the accomplishment of a given task.

competency (simple reproduction-type): competency which requires the execution of a known plan in the accomplishment of a given task.

competency: capability of a person to accomplish a given task. A competency may also be seen as a set of declarative and procedural knowledge stored in long-term memory that is activated by a plan generator in the accomplishment of a given task.

complex task: task whose accomplishment requires the execution of a large number of operations.

concept: cognitive unit that allows a person to represent an object or thing. Concepts are values assigned to the variables of a schema. A concept may be general or particular.

congruent question (to a learning objective): a question that elicits the performance described in a given objective.

constructivism: school of thought which considers that new knowledge is built up from knowledge already possessed instead of being a direct copy of some external reality.

content of instructional activities: set of declaratives and/or procedures and/or attitudes that instructional activities intend to convey.

course goal: a statement that entails all the competencies a given course is supposed to help one acquire (synonym: general objective).

course organization: one of the steps of the instructional design and development process. It consists of the formulation of learning objectives of an instructional delivery system.

course: set of lessons leading to a desired knowledge state.

declarative knowledge: type of knowledge that allows the representation of objects and events. Concepts, propositions, and episodes are examples of declarative knowledge.

deep structure: (from linguistics) underlying meaning of the words.

desired state or situation (also goal state): desired state of reality a person is hoping to attain with the accomplishment of a given task.

emotion: the outcome of physiological and psychological processes; feelings that are positive or negative depending upon the person's cognitive evaluation and physiological reaction.

encoding: mental process involving the registration of information onto the neural networks of the human brain.

equilibrium: state of an organism in which its needs are satisfied.

expectancy: representation of what a person will be able to do after learning; representation of a situation, a state, or a goal that a person wants to attain; representation of a situation or a state into which the needs of a person could be satisfied.

expert system: computerized information processing system that imitates the behavior of a human being while solving a problem.

formative evaluation: evaluation providing feedback for revision. More specifically, it is a step of the instructional design and development process involving the tryout of a prototype with a target population in order to make improvements.

function for the generation of plans: set of procedures used in the elaboration of plans.

function: (computer science) set of procedures.

general objective: (see course goal).

heuristics: rule of thumb or set of higher order rules used in the search for solutions to problems (synonyms: cognitive strategy, problem-solving strategy).

hierarchization of action: cognitivist principle that suggests the planning and the execution of action generally occur in a hierarchical order from plans-generation to their concretization in action.

information processing system: set of structures and functions that allows a person to accomplish tasks. The information processing system of a person allows him or her to stay adapted to the environment.

information processing: execution of operations on symbolic data in the accomplishment of a task. It may be accomplished mentally or on a computer.

initial state or situation: state of the reality a person confronts prior to the accomplishment of a given task.

instructional delivery system: set of instructional activities with which a learner interacts in order to acquire one or several competencies.

instructional designer: the person responsible for the design of instructional delivery systems (synonyms: designer, training consultant, instructional technologist).

instructional event: event which activates the mental processes related to the acquiring of a competency.

instructional method: set of instructional events that supports the acquiring of a competency or set of competencies.

instructional methods selection: a step of the instructional design and development process consisting of the determination of appropriate instructional events for the attainment of given objectives.

instructional systems design: a step-by-step process leading to the design of a full instructional system.

instructional technology: set of processes and devices used to facilitate learning. Also, more specifically, a systematic process for the development of instruction.

instructor: a person who assists a learner in accomplishing a learning task.

knowledge representation (process): activity into which a person is engaged when building a representation of reality.

knowledge: information integrated to schemas that enables understanding and action.

learning objective: statement which describes a targeted performance.

learning task, size of: the amount of information processing that a learner must invest to acquire one or several competencies.

learning: process in which a person engages in order to acquire competencies and/or attitudes.

lesson: a relatively small set of learning activities that enable the acquiring of competencies.

linguistics: one of the cognitive sciences; its goal is the study of human language functioning.

media: devices and instructional materials that convey the instructional events of a given instructional method.

memory, long-term: "place" in the brain where cognitive units are stored permanently.

memory, short-term: "place" in the brain where mental operations are executed and where the outcomes of these operations are stored for a very short time (seconds or minutes).

memory: support that permits the storing and the conservation of information. There are at least two types of memory: long-term memory and short-term memory.

mental image: cognitive unit that allows a person to represent a part of concrete reality.

mental model: the internal representation that a person has of a given system.

mental process: set of operations executed in the accomplishment of a given task.

modularity: cognitivist principle that considers the accomplishment of a complex task as the result of the working of modules or complementary functions.

motivation: effort that a person is ready to invest for the accomplishment of a given task.

motor function: set of procedures that is used in the execution of physical actions.

neuron: cell of the nervous system that ensures the passage of signals which allow the encoding of information.

neuroscience: one of the cognitive sciences; its object is the understanding of intelligent behavior by the study of the physiological mechanisms of the brain.

operation function: set of procedures used in the execution of arithmetic and/or logical operations.

operation: component of a production rule, a procedure, or a heuristic that makes a transformation possible.

perception: activity in which an information processing system is engaged when constructing representations of input stimuli.

perceptual function: set of procedures used for the representation of external stimuli and for the building of declarative and/or procedural knowledge.

performance: behavior made possible by the mastery of a competency.

philosophy: the search for truth through logical reasoning, one of the cognitive sciences; one of its goals consists of the study of human thought.

plan: representation that guides the activity of a person while accomplishing a given task.

planning: activity in which a person is engaged while elaborating a plan.

plan generator: (see function for the generation of plans).

post-test: test administered at the end of instructional activities in order to assess the mastery of competencies taught. Comparing the results of trainees on the post-test with those on the **pre-test** allows one to determine the effectiveness of the instruction.

prerequisites: knowledge and skills necessary for new knowledge and skills to be acquired.

pre-test: test administered at the beginning of instructional activities in order to establish the degree of mastery of the competencies that will be taught.

problem solving: process a person uses to search for solution to a problem.

procedural knowledge: type of knowledge that allows a person to act upon reality (*i.e.*, "know-how"). Productions, procedures and heuristics are examples of procedural knowledge.

procedure: set of production rules used in the accomplishment of a given task.

production rule: cognitive unit of the form: "if ... then" used for the transformation of a given state into another one.

proposition: a cognitive unit that expresses a relationship between a set of concepts.

prototype: first version of an instructional delivery system.

refinement: last phase in the acquisition of a competency. This phase generally follows the assembly of the competency. Its goal is the shaping or tuning of the competency.

relationship: component that associates concepts or other cognitive units.

representation (structure): mnemonic structure that allows a person to figure out reality or act upon it.

retrieval: mental process that permits the search and retrieval of information from long-term memory.

schema (plural schemas or schemata): generic structure of knowledge that enables a person to represent reality and/or act upon it. A schema is made of variables and relations and/or operations.

script: cognitive unit used to represent events, processes, principles. It is made of an interrelated set of propositions.

specific objective: a statement that describes the performance made possible by the mastery of a competency. The statement contains an action verb that describes the performance, a description of an initial and of desired state, indications about the type of competency that has to be acquired, and minimum criteria of performance.

storing of information: mental process that consists of the encoding of information into long-term memory with the intent of subsequent retrieval.

structuring of the subject matter: process by which cognitive units and attitudes are organized in order to facilitate their acquisition.

surface structure: (from linguistics) words that are used to communicate ideas.

table of instructional contents: summary organization of declarative and procedural knowledge in order to facilitate learning.

task accomplishment: activity necessary to change a given situation or state into a desired situation or goal state.

terminal objective: instructional objective that is the convergent point of other objectives.

test construction: one step in the design and development of an instructional system. It refers to the building of tools that enable the assessment of competencies that have been taught.

test of prerequisites: test administered at the beginning of instructional activities in order to verify if the learner possesses the cognitive units on top of which new knowledge and skills will be built (as contrasted with "pre-test," which measures prior knowledge of content to be learned).

test: assessment tool used to establish the learning of a competency. A valid test is made up of questions congruent to learning objectives.

training needs analysis: a step in the instructional design and development process, involving the identification of the competencies that should be taught to a target population.

training program: set of instructional activities. A training program generally consists of sets of courses.

training session: set of instructional activities that enables a person to acquire competencies.

understanding: mental process which consists of making sense out of given information. Schemas allow the understanding of information.

variables (of a schema):   component(s) of a schema that may take diverse values.

verbal function: set of procedures involving words; used in oral or written communication.

Answers to Questions for Review

Chapter 1

(1) The basic response is to search for a plan that will fill the gap. The four prerequisites are: to be able to represent to himself the current situation and the desired one, to be able to accomplish tasks, to acquire competencies, and to be motivated to acquire these competencies to accomplish such tasks.

(2) With accurate mental models, both designers and teachers are in a better position to motivate the learner, to help him to store information, to form representations, and to use the information.

Chapter 2

(1) Each of these situations suggests a need that may be satisfied by accomplishing a given task. Remember that several needs may be met by accomplishing the same task: (a) John and Betty want to satisfy physiological needs (hunger); (b) Peter probably accomplishes this task in order to satisfy his need for love and belonging; (c) Mary probably satisfies her need for self-actualization; (d) Paul and Joan probably satisfy their need to give and receive love. (They could also be satisfying needs for social approval as well as security in their old age).

(2) An expectancy is the mental representation of a situation in which a need will potentially be satisfied. A need is what causes this representation to occur.

(3) Review the model in Figure 2 for applicability to your situation.

(4)   Use tournaments or educational games to build competition (leading to self-esteem from pride in accomplishment), use learning in pairs or small groups to build upon social needs, and use the project method for self-expression and (for group projects) social needs.

(5)   Positive: pride in accomplishment, enthusiasm, enjoyment. Negative: anxiety, weariness. To enhance the positive ones, work for variety in teaching methods, and a sense of humor. The learning environment should be a pleasant place to be. To diminish anxiety, provide clear expectations for desired performance. To diminish weariness and boredom, increase variety.

(6)   See Glossary for "motivation." Motivation to learn is the effort one is ready to invest to accomplish a learning task.

(7)   A few of these are: (a) size of perceived need; (b) the perceived size of the learning task; and (c) feelings of self-efficacy, i.e., how likely the learner feels he or she is succeeding at the given learning task.

Chapter 3

(1)   The basic cognitive unit is a schema.

(2)   See Chapter 3 or the Glossary.

(3)   A schema is a generic structure of knowledge; it has variables to which values may be assigned. A schema is used to represent several instances. A specific element of knowledge lacks such variables; it represents only *one* instance.

(4)   Suppose that the title, "The Laundry," had been provided to you before the reading of this text. Could that have made a difference in your understanding and being able to remember? This text is hard to understand because you do not have an integrative schema to assimilate the various concepts and propositions given. A title of the text would have provided you with just such a schema for receiving this information. You have schemas that enable you to

understand the specific concepts and propositions of this text, but you do not have a schema into which these concepts and propositions may be integrated as a whole. When it is time to remember this text, you cannot use such a schema to help you retrieve these various concepts and propositions.

(5) There are mainly two types of knowledge: declarative and procedural. For Anderson, particularly with adults, declarative knowledge is acquired first, and then comes procedural knowledge.

(6) From the diagram in Figure 6, we see that concepts and propositions must precede the learning rules of production. Lower level schemas must precede learning higher level, organizing schemas. And, finally, reproduction-type competency requires all elements leading to rules of production plus episodes and procedures.

Chapter 4

(1) The list of ingredients tells you about the current situation; the picture describes the desired situation or goal state; and the recipe gives the list of steps (the plan) to follow in order to change the current situation into the desired one.

(2) Each of these functions involves several parts of the brain. However, the principal components involved are: (a) affective—reticular activation system; (b) perceptual—the occipital lobe, the sensory areas, the parietal lobes, and the left temporal lobe; and (c) the execution of plans—the frontal lobes.

(3) The processing will occur in a definite sequence. For example, your car has a blowout on the highway. You will represent the current and the desire situations with your perceptual function; the plan generator will suggest ways of solving the problem; and your motor function will control your action if you should decide to change the tire yourself. Alternatively, if you have decided to telephone for help, you will use your verbal function. The hierarchical aspect of

this functioning results from the plan generating function's "giving orders" to the other brain functions.

(4)   A competency is the capacity a person has to accomplish a given task. As this capacity is exercised, task accomplishment occurs.

Chapter 5

(1)   Knowledge is the "knowing that" and the "know how" that is in long-term memory. Working competency is the activating of this knowledge by the plan generator. Performance is the external result of this activation. Using the computer as an illustration, the knowledge is the program and data structures that are stored in the memory of the computer. When these programs are running, we refer to the working competencies. What you see happening on your screen or on your printer as the result of information processing is the output or performance.

(2)   A person that has a competency of the reproduction-type knows the plan for the accomplishment of a given task. A person that has a competency of the production-type has to devise a plan. Programming a computer requires a competency of the production-type. Executing a program requires a competency of the reproduction-type.

(3)   (a) John is evaluating competencies of the production type (PO); (b) the learners will have competencies of the reproduction type (RV). Obviously, there is a mismatch between the competencies provided by instruction and those required by testing.

(4)   The competencies would be classified as follows:
   (a)   RO, since the actor knows the plan, and has to execute abstract operations.
   (b)   RM, if the typist has to type a text from a handwritten one.
   (c)   RM
   (d)   PV, if the learner has to elaborate a plan for writing this biography.
   (e)   RV, if the learner knows the steps of the process.

(f) POV

(g) PO

Chapter 6

(1) There are three phases in the acquisition of a competency. During the **motivation phase** the learner elaborates chain(s) of expectancies. The person foresees the pay-off of the learning task to be accomplished. During the **assembly phase**, the learner works on building the competency, encoding of the declarative and procedural aspects of the competency. During the **refinement phase**, the learner is engaged in making the competency more precise.

As an example, John has decided to learn a foreign language. By doing this, John understands that it will be easier to travel in countries where the language is spoken. He will also be able to read books and to watch movies produced in the foreign language. John then attends courses in this foreign language. For each specific competency, he encodes the declarative part of it by being exposed in one way or another to the particularities of this foreign language. He also has to practice (encoding of the procedural part). Then John works on the refinement of his competencies by engaging in activities such as talking to people who speak this language. This refinement may take years.

(2) They are encoding of the declarative and procedural aspects.

(3) While learning by accretion, the learner already has a schema that accounts for the information presented. While learning by restructuring, the learner lacks an adequate schema to account for the information presented to him. In this case the learner has to modify an already existing schema or to combine other schemas to form a new one.

(4) The phase of assembly is only partially supported, and the refinement phase is not supported at all. Only the encoding of the declarative part of the competency is occurring, since there are no

opportunities for practice. To complete the training, he could use simulations, role playing or demonstration by the learner in a real setting.

Chapter 7

(1)   See Figure 15, Systematic design of instruction, for an overview of this process.

(2)   These activities occur: (a) while organizing the course; (b) while selecting instructional methods and media; (c) while analyzing the objectives; (d) while pilot testing.

Chapter 8

(1)   The precision with which the subject matter is treated; the attention given to assembling and refining competencies; the provision of feedback to the learner—to name a few.

Index

About the Authors

Robert Brien is Professor of Instructional Technology at Laval University, Quebec, Canada. He holds an undergraduate degree in Science and a Masters in Instructional Technology from Laval University, with a doctorate in Instructional Systems Design from Florida State University. Having authored numerous articles and conducted many workshops, he has worked internationally as a consultant for the Food and Agricultural Organization (FAO) of the United Nations. He completed a sabbatical year as a Visiting Scholar at the Center for Human Information Processing at the University of California, San Diego. His academic interests include cognitive science, instructional design, and the selection of appropriate methods of instruction.

Nick Eastmond is Professor of Instructional Technology with an adjunct appointment in the Department of Languages and Philosophy at Utah State University, Logan, Utah. He holds a Bachelor of Arts degree in Economics from the University of Utah, a Masters in Elementary Education from Ohio University, and a doctorate in Educational Psychology from the University of Utah. He spent a sabbatical year at the World Center for Computers in Paris, France and a year as a Visiting Professor in Foreign Languages at the United States Air Force Academy. His current academic interests are program evaluation, qualitative methods, and the use of technology for foreign language learning.